It was on the way to Izzie's that I saw Him.

We were driving through Highgate past St. Michael's school, and he was coming out of the gates with another boy. . . . A ten-out-of ten, a face like Leonardo DiCaprio's, but he was taller with olive skin and dark hair. Absolutely drop dead goooorgeousissimo.

I watched him walk away down the pavement on the other side. It was like time stood still, and suddenly I understood what all the fuss is about. Usually I never see boys I like. . . . Not like him. . . . I wonder who he is? I must find out. I'll persuade Izzie to come up to Highgate to hang out. There are loads of cafés there. He must go into one of them sometimes after school, all the St. Michael's boys do. My heart was racing.

It had happened. At last. Love at first sight.

As we drove on, I felt elated. I had a goal: Meet that boy.

Mates, Dates, and Inflatable Bras

Cathy Hopkins

Simon Pulse

New York   London   Toronto   Sydney   Singapore

First Simon Pulse edition February 2003

Text copyright © 2001 by Cathy Hopkins
Originally Published in Great Britain in 2001
by Piccadilly Press Ltd.

SIMON PULSE
An imprint of Simon & Schuster
Children's Publishing Division
1230 Avenue of the Americas
New York, NY 10020

Designed by Debra Sfetsios
The text of this book was set in Bembo.

Printed in the United States of America
6 8 10 9 7 5

Library of Congress Control Number: 2002106131

ISBN 0-689-85544-3

For Rachel

*(And thanks to Rachel, Grace, Natalie, Emily, Isobel, and Laura
for letting me know what's hot and what's not. And thanks to
Jude and Brenda at Piccadilly for their input and for giving me
a chance to be fourteen again. And last but not least,
thanks to the lovely Rosemary Bromley.)*

Mates, Dates, and Inflatable Bras

Chapter 1

What Makes Me "Me"?

If she picks me out in class again, I shall scream.

Wacko Watkins. That's what I call her. Our new teacher. We've got her for PE first period this morning, worse luck.

"I wonder what kind of weird project she's got lined up to torture us with this week," I said as we hurried down the corridor to get to our classroom before second bell.

"She's okay as teachers go," said Izzie. "She makes you think about stuff. And she seems really interested in what we feel. I like her lessons."

"Well I don't," I said. "It's bad enough having a mum who's a shrink without getting it at school as well. I get that 'let's all share our feelings' stuff at home. I wish Watkins would give me a break here. She always singles me out."

"Probably because you're quiet in class. She's trying to find out what's going on in that daft head of yours. You're lucky. At least your mum and dad bother to ask what's going on. All mine care about are my marks. Whether I get A, B, or C. I think I'd faint from shock if either of them ever asked how I actually *felt* about anything."

Izzie's my best mate. Or was. I'm not sure anymore. Not since Nesta Williams arrived at the end of last term. Izzie and I have hung out together since middle school. It's always been me and Izzie. Izzie and me. Sharing everything. Clothes. Makeup. CDs. Secrets. And then along comes Nesta, and I reckon it's two's company, three's a crowd. But I seem to be the only one who sees it that way. I'm going to have to tackle Izzie about it, but I rarely get her on her own these days.

"Hurry along and take your places, girls," called

Miss Watkins, coming up behind us.

I hope she hadn't heard what I said about her.

Miss Watkins is a bit odd looking. Make that very odd looking. She looks like she put a finger in an electric socket. Her expression is always startled, like a cartoon character who's seen something shocking and their eyes pop out. She's as thin as a wire, and her hair's frizzy grey, coiling out at all angles.

"Okay, girls, now settle down," she said. "We've got a lot to talk about today."

Here we go. Talk. Talk. Let's talk. I wish we could read today. Quietly. Or write. Quietly. Why do we have to talk? Doesn't anyone realize I'm going through a quiet-but-mysterious phase? Like Geri when she split from the Spice Girls.

As Wacko perched on the corner of her desk and hitched her skirt up, we all got an eyeful of her pale legs above knee-high stockings. She has skin like Saran Wrap. Transparent. You can see all the veins underneath it. Enough to bring up your breakfast first thing in the morning, I can tell you.

"There's a few things I want you to start thinking about for the rest of the term," she continued. "As you probably know, it's soon going to be time to choose your subjects for next year. Which ones you want to do."

Inwardly I groaned. I've been dreading this. See, I don't know. Haven't a clue. Not the faintest.

"I know it's a lot to think about and I don't want any of you to panic or feel pressurised. We've plenty of time, that's why I want you to give it some attention now so it doesn't come as a big rush later on."

Too late, I thought. I'm already in major panic mode.

"I want you to think about your future. Your goals. Ambitions. What you want to be when you're older. Right, anybody got any ideas?"

She started to look round the class so I put my head down and tried to become invisible.

"Lucy?"

I knew. See. I knew it would be me she asked first.

"Yes, miss?"

"Let's get the ball rolling. Any idea what you'd like to do?"

I could feel myself going red as everyone turned to look at me.

Duhhh? I dunno. Doctor. Nah. Too much blood. Dentist. Nah. Fiddling about in people's mouths all day. Yuk. Vet? *Yes*. Vet. I love animals. After Izzie, Ben and Jerry, our Labradors, are my next best friends. So, vet? I could be on all those animal rescue programs on telly, looking glam as I save poor animals. Maybe not. Ben stood on a piece of glass last week. I almost fainted when the vet said he'd have to have a few stitches in his paw. I couldn't watch. Had to leave the room like a right sissy. He was fine after but I can't bear to see an animal in pain. So probably not the best career choice. So what else? What?

"Don't know, miss," I blurted out, wishing she'd choose someone else.

"No idea at all?" she asked.

I shook my head.

Candice Carter put her hand up. She was bursting.

Thankfully Wacko turned to her.

"Candice?"

"Lifeguard, Miss Watkins."

"Lifeguard. Now that's an original one. And why do you want to be a lifeguard?"

"So I can give all the boys the kiss of life, miss."

Everyone cracked up laughing. She's such a tart, Candice Carter.

"Anyone got any more sensible suggestions?" asked Miss Watkins, looking round.

By now, half the class had their hands up.

"Writer," said Mary O'Connor.

"Nurse," said Joanne Richards.

"Air hostess," said Gabby Jones.

"TV presenter," said Jade Wilcocks.

"Hairdresser," said Mo Harrison.

"Rich and famous," said Nesta, and everyone laughed again.

Everyone knows what they want to do. Everyone. But me.

I'm fourteen. Everyone's always saying, "Oh don't grow up too fast" and "Enjoy your youth," now suddenly it's, "What're you going to do with the rest of your life?"

"Excellent," said Miss Watkins. "Those who know what they want to do are lucky. And those who don't," she looked pointedly at me, "don't worry. You don't have to decide today. But it does help to have some inkling of what direction you might like to go in when it comes to choosing your subjects later. For those of you who don't know, we'll have a look at it all over the next few weeks. In fact a good starting point is to take a look at who you are now. Identify your strengths and weaknesses. The seeds of today are the fruits of tomorrow. The thoughts of today are the actions of tomorrow. So, to start with, I'm going to give you an essay to be handed in at the end of term. Doesn't have to be too long. A page or so."

She picked up her chalk and turned to the blackboard.

What makes me "me"? she wrote.

"That's your title. I'll give you fifteen minutes now to make a few notes."

She wrote a few more questions up on the board.

Who am I?

What are my interests?

What do I want? What are my goals in life?

What are my strengths and weaknesses?

What would I like to do as a career?

For the last part of the lesson, I could see everyone scribbling madly.

I knew what Izzie would be writing. She wants to be a singer. Has since we were nine. She writes all her own songs and plays guitar. She wants to be the next Alanis Morissette. She even looks like her now. She's got the same long dark hair and she wears the same hippie dippie clothes. Not my taste, but they suit Iz.

I glanced across at Nesta. She was writing frantically as well. Typical. She's so sure of herself and where she's going. She wants to be a model and will probably get there. She's totally gorgeous-looking. Her dad's Italian so she's got his straight black hair, like silk right down to her waist, and her mum's Jamaican so she's got her dark skin and eyes. She could easily be Naomi Campbell's younger sister. Tall and skinny with an amazing pixie face.

I wish I were black. They have the best skin, even when they're old. Like Nesta's mum. I've seen her on television. She reads the news on cable. She's ancient, at least forty, but she only looks about twenty. I'm the typical "English rose," pale, blond, and boring. I'd rather be a tropical flower, like Nesta, all exotic and colorful.

I stared at the blank piece of paper in front of me.

What makes me "me"? I began to write.

I'm small and don't look my age. People always think I'm in Year Seven or Eight.

I stared out of the window hoping for inspiration. Jobs for little people. Maybe I could audition to be one of the Munchkins if they ever remake *The Wizard of Oz*? They're tiny. Or Mini Me in the next Austin Powers movie.

And what are you going to be when you grow up, Nesta? Model.

And you, Izzie? Singer-songwriter.

Lucy? Mini Me.

Yeah. Right. Now I'm being plain stupid. I must have some decent ideas locked in my brain somewhere.

I made myself concentrate. What makes me "me"?

I'm the youngest in my family.

Fifteen minutes later and that was all I'd written.

"Just before the bell goes," said Miss Watkins, "I'd like to give you all a profile sheet to fill out.

Purely for yourselves to help get you started if you're stuck. Nobody needs to see them, they're only for you, to get you thinking along different lines."

I looked at the sheet of paper she handed me.

Help. I'm usually good at essays and stuff. But this time I haven't a clue. I don't know who I am. Or what makes me "me."

Or what I'm going to do when I grow up.

Or where I fit.

Profile Sheet

Name: Lucy Lovering

Physical

Age: 14 but I look about 12.

Height/build: 4 foot 8 and a *HALF*. Slim,
  30 minus A chest. My brothers call me Nancy
  no tits. Not funny.

Coloring: blond hair, blue eyes.

Sociology

Parents' occupations: Mum's a shrink
  (psychotherapist), Dad runs the local health
  shop and is a part-time musician.

Education: favorite subjects: Art, English
  worst subjects: anything else.

Home life: two elder brothers: Steve (17) he's
  a computer whiz, Lal (15) he's sad, spotty,
  and humungously gross but thinks he's God's
  gift. Two dogs: Ben and Jerry.

Race/nationality: English/Scottish. Possibly alien.

Hobbies: reading, magazines, old movies, TV,
  sewing.

Psychology

Ambitions: good question.

Frustrations/disappointments:

- my parents, who are a pair of old hippies.
- Mum and Dad always ramming herbal teas and health products down my neck when I'm quite happy with chips and burgers.
- Mum's obsession with recycling and buying clothes from charity shops.
- the fact I'm so small.
- the fact my best friend now appears to be Nesta Williams's best friend.

Temperament: I think I may be going mental.

Qualities: sense of humor, a good best friend when allowed to be.

Abilities/talents: good listener, good at drawing.

Chapter 2

Angel
Cards

When I got home after school I did what I always do. Headed for the fridge.

"When the going gets tough . . ." I said.

"The tough eat ice cream," finished Izzie, swooping in and taking the tub from the freezer.

"Diet again on Monday," said Nesta.

I can't believe she diets. She's as thin as a rake.

By five o'clock our kitchen was packed. Me, Izzie, and Nesta tucking into bowls of pecan nut fudge. Brothers Steve and Laurence plus two of their schoolmates, Matthew and Tom, all busy cutting mammoth hunks of bread then slapping on peanut butter and honey. Yuk. Mum making a cup of tea. Herbal of course. And Dad attempting to feed Ben and Jerry who are more interested in my ice cream than dog food.

It's chaos in here.

"Why did you call them Ben and Jerry?" asked Nesta, pointing at the dogs—Ben, who had his paws up on my knees trying to get his nose in my bowl, and Jerry, looking longingly at Izzie in the hope she'd take pity and give him a taste. I gave Ben the last spoonful to lick; I'm a sucker for his great sad eyes and that pathetic "no one ever feeds me" look of his, plus he's still got his paw in a bandage, poor thing.

"We named them after they ate a whole tub of Ben and Jerry's Chunky Monkey when they were puppies," said Lal through a mouthful of bread. "They love ice cream."

I think Lal fancies Nesta, he's gone all creepy and over-friendly since she walked in. He keeps flicking his hair back and giving her meaningful looks. I don't think she's even noticed. He likes to imagine himself as a ladies' man. Ever since Tracy

Marcuson next door let him snog her last Christmas. He's not bad-looking in a kind of Matt Damon way, but I don't think Nesta would be interested. She likes older boys or so she says. And not that she'd fancy my eldest brother Steve either. He's seventeen and a bit too swotty-looking for her, though he's quite nice looking when he takes his glasses off and has a decent haircut. But he's not bothered about girls, unlike Casanova Lal; Steve prefers computers and books.

"It's like Waterloo station in here," sighed Mum, clearing a space at the table. She doesn't mind though. Our house is always full of people, usually all piled in the kitchen, which is the largest room in the house. Dad knocked a wall through last year to open it up a bit, and though we do have more space now, he ran out of money so couldn't finish the job.

"What are those marks on the wall?" asked Nesta, pointing to some pencil marks by the fridge.

"Our heights as we were growing up," said Lal, getting up and going to stand against the wall to show her how it worked. "See, on every birthday we measure how much we've grown with a pencil mark." He pointed to the highest. "Those are Steve's."

"And these must be Lucy's," said Nesta, looking at the shortest marks. She stood at least six inches higher than I had last birthday.

She then had a close look at our "original" wallpaper. To cover up for the lack of it, Steve, Lal, and I have plastered our artwork from school all over one wall. And Mum, who's convinced that one day Dad will actually get round to decorating, has used another area to try out different color paint samples.

"Very *Vogue* interior," Nesta smiled as she examined Mum's wall, which looks like a patchwork quilt of misshapen daubs in various shades of yellow, blue, terra-cotta, and green.

"Not," I said.

I haven't been to Nesta's house yet, but Izzie has and says it's amazing. Straight out of an interior design mag. Still, Nesta doesn't seem bothered by our lack of decor style. In fact she appears to like it here, as she comes back most nights after school now. Her mum works different shifts as a newsreader on the telly and her dad's a film director so he's often away shooting. Nesta has an older brother as well but she says he's hardly ever at home either.

Izzie has always come home with me, ever since I've known her. Her mum and stepdad don't get home from work until after seven so it was arranged ages ago that she'd come here until one of them picks her up.

Izzie says I have to give Nesta a chance and get to know her properly, but I'm not sure how I feel about her being here all the time. It's like, first she moves in on my best friend, and now she's moving in on my family. I'm trying to be friends and I do sort of like her—it's hard not to, she's great fun—but I can't help feeling pushed out. Everyone loves Nesta when they meet her. She's so confident and pretty.

It all started a few weeks ago when Izzie came to find me after school. She looked out of breath as if she had been running.

"Can Nesta come back with us to yours?" she asked, looking behind her as though someone was following.

She saw me hesitate.

"She needs friends," she said. "She's not as sure of herself as she makes out. I know she acts all tough, like she doesn't need anyone or care what anyone thinks of her but I just found her at the bus

17

stop, crying. That creep Josie Riley and her mates have been calling her names, and she doesn't want to go home until her mum's back. I don't want to leave her there on her own.'

I'd have felt mean refusing and I did feel sorry for her. I know what those bullies in Year Eleven can be like.

"Yeah. Tell her to come," I said. "That is if she doesn't mind my mad family."

Course Mum and Dad made her welcome straight away. They always do with people. They may not have enough money to paint the kitchen walls but they don't seem to mind feeding the neighborhood. Love, peace, and have a chunk of organic bread. That's what they live by. Share what you have. The world is just a great big family.

Because Dad runs the local health shop we're fed all sorts of weird stuff. All organic, preservative free. Tastes okay though. But some nights I don't know what I'm eating. Tahini. Gomasio. Miso. And herbal teas. Disgusting. Especially chamomile. Smells like cats' pee. What I'd give for a McDonald's followed by a big fat chocolate milkshake. But no, Mum and Dad are veggies so the only burger you get round here is the tofu variety and milkshakes are made of soy.

Izzie says it's one of the things she likes best about Mum and Dad, but then she's into all that stuff as well. New Age, alternative.

"I wish my parents were cool like yours," she said once. "They really care about stuff. The environment. What we put in our bodies. They're not like usual boring parents."

"Exactly," I said. "I used to love the way they were when I was younger, but I wish Mum would look a bit, well, a bit more bland these days."

"Why?" said Izzie. "I think she looks brilliant."

"Brilliant?" I said. Not a word that would spring to my mind when describing Mum's style. Peculiar more like.

"I love a bargain," Mum's always saying. "Which is why I shop at all the charity shops. You get a good class of cast-off in North London."

Mostly I don't mind, but last month's parents' meeting was the worst. I wanted her to look normal for once, but she came down the stairs ready to go, wearing red-and-white-striped tights, a purply tweed skirt, *and* a green checked jacket. She has no sense of color coordination at all and slings it all together with total disregard for what mixes and matches.

"What do you think?" she asked, giving me a twirl.

"Er, very colorful," I said, thinking fast. "But why not try your green jacket with some navy trousers? Or maybe the purple skirt with a grey or blue shirt? That would look nice."

"But I love the tights," said Mum. "I have to wear them."

"Well how about with a plain black dress?" I suggested. "And you could accessorize the red and white stripes with red and white bracelets?"

She sort of listened. *Sort of.* She went upstairs and changed into a black dress. Then threw a multi-colored poncho that looks like an old blanket over it. And, of course, she was *still* wearing the red-and-white tights. I give up. Everyone was staring at her when we got to school. She stood out among all the other mums in their Marks and Spencer's navy and white. Even her hair is different. Most mums have the standard short haircut, but Mum's is really long, halfway down her back. Too long for her age, I think, though it does look okay when she puts it back in a plait.

Then again it could have been the car that people were looking at that evening. We've had the same one for years. I think Mum and Dad bought it at university, which is where they first met. It's a Volkswagon Beetle. And for some reason Dad painted it bright turquoise. No, you definitely can't miss it amongst the Range Rovers and BMWs.

Dad dresses pretty normally. Cords and jumpers. I mean, he doesn't exactly have to dress smart to dole out people's muesli at the shop, but I wish he'd get rid of the ponytail. Does he listen? No. According to a mag I read, balding men compensate by having a ponytail. Poor Dad. It must be awful losing his hair, but it would look so much better if he had what little he has left cropped short.

"So how was school today?" he asked the assorted chomping faces in the kitchen.

"Mmphhh, okay, fine," came the reply.

"What have you been doing?" he asked, turning to me.

"Career choices, course choices," said Nesta, butting in. "Making decisions."

And that set them all off again. Even Lal, Steve, Matthew, and Tom joined in.

"I want to be a record producer," said Lal.

"I want to play in a band," said Tom, getting up and playing air guitar.

"I want to be an inventor," said Steve.

It was a repeat of the morning at school with everyone knowing what they want to be except me. I could see Mum looking at me as everyone babbled away.

"What about you, Lucy?" she asked. "What do you want to be?"

I shrugged. "Dunno."

Izzie and Nesta burst in with their brilliant career plans, and I could see Mum was watching me with concern as they enthused away. She doesn't miss a trick. She winked at me when no one was looking.

"The longest journey starts with the first step," she said.

Steve, Lal, and I groaned. We're used to her coming out with her "quote for the day." In her work as a psychotherapist she spends loads of time with people who are fed up with their lives in one way or another so she's always looking for new things to say to them to cheer them up a bit. She reads all the latest self-help books and likes to pass on words of wisdom to the rest of us.

"Okay, who wants an Angel Card?" she asked.

"Oh, *Mum*," I said, feeling embarrassed, "I'm *sure* no one's interested."

"What's an Angel Card?" asked Izzie enthusiastically.

"A box of cards I bought last week to use in my counselling sessions," said Mum. "I haven't got round to taking them into work yet. Each card has a quote written on it."

She got up and found her pack.

"You pick one," she said, shuffling the cards and selecting one, "and let it speak to you."

"*The darkest hour is just before dawn*," she read, then handed the cards to Izzie. "Your turn, Iz."

Izzie loves stuff like this. Tarot cards, astrology, I Ching. She took a card and read out, "*Choice not chance determines destiny.*"

"Very sensible," said Dad. "Better to choose what you want than let it all drift by you and end up doing something you don't really want to do."

I started to feel panicky again. Was that going to happen to me because I didn't know what to choose? I'd just drift along in a haze of confusion?

Suddenly I felt a cold, wet nose pushing against my hand. Ben's dopey face gazed up at me from under the table as if to say he understood. Sometimes I think dogs are psychic.

Izzie handed the pack to Nesta. "You choose one."

Nesta picked and read, "*The tragedy in life doesn't lie in not reaching your goal. The tragedy lies in having no goal.*"

Arggghhhh. It was getting worse. I have no goal. It's a tragedy.

"That's okay," continued Nesta. "I've got a goal. Clothes Show in a few weeks. I get spotted by talent scout and become a super-duper supermodel"

Lal's jaw dropped even more as he goggled at Nesta. "A supermodel? You'll get picked easy." The creep.

Nesta handed the cards to me and I let my hand hover, then shuffled. Let it be a good one, I prayed, let it be a good one.

I picked one out. "*Don't wait for your ship to come in*," I read. "*Swim out to it.*"

"Good one," said Dad.

Psychic Ben clearly liked the card as well. He tried to jump up on my knee to lick my face. Seeing as he's an enormous thing, he almost knocked me flying, making everyone laugh.

"Down, Ben," I said. "You know I love you but you're too heavy."

Reluctantly he got down but sank his head on to my lap and refused to budge it.

I read my card again. Right, I thought. I'll be positive. I'll swim out to the ship. Right. I will. But how?

Once again Mum clocked my anxious expression. She squeezed my hand. "There's no hurry, you know. You don't have to decide what you want to be this minute."

I knew she meant well, but I thought the sooner I swam out to my ship the better.

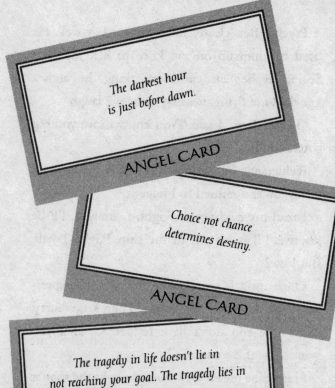

The darkest hour
is just before dawn.

ANGEL CARD

Choice not chance
determines destiny.

ANGEL CARD

The tragedy in life doesn't lie in
not reaching your goal. The tragedy lies in
having no goal.

ANGEL CARD

Don't wait for your ship to come in.
Swim out to it.

ANGEL CARD

Chapter 3

Girls'
Night Out

Saturday night. Girls' night out.

We're going to go to the Hollywood Bowl in Finchley. Dad calls it teen paradise. Everyone from our school hangs out there. It's a huge complex with a bowling alley, cafés, and a cinema, all built round a square where you can park if you have a car or stand about looking cool if you want to be seen. At the weekend, this is most of the teenage population of North London.

Speaking of which, what am I going to wear? Nesta and Izzie always look fab so I'd better make an effort.

I rifled through my wardrobe, but all that stared back at me were last year's oddments, worn out, boring, or babyish. I had a pink phase for a while but it looks too girlie girlie now. I really need some new clothes.

Suddenly I had an idea.

"Mum," I called down the stairs. "Where did you put that pile of stuff from Oxfam?"

"In the hall cupboard," she called from the kitchen. "I thought you didn't want any of it."

Mum had arrived back this morning from her weekly shop with the usual carrier bag of Oxfam bargains. I wouldn't be seen dead in most of it, too big or too patterned, but there was one shirt: size twenty. I don't know who Mum thought was going to wear it and initially I cast it aside. But it was nice fabric, silver and silky.

I pulled it out of the bag, got a large pair of scissors and went to the sewing machine in the sitting room. I cut off the sleeves and the front panels, leaving me with the back. I cut it down, hemmed the bottom then set about shaping the top and sides.

In under an hour, I'd finished. Posh Spice, eat

your heart out, I thought as I tried on my new handkerchief halter top. It didn't look half bad either. I could wear it with my black jeans.

"You're not going out in that," said Dad as I modeled my top for the family. "It's October, you'll freeze to death."

"I'll take a jacket," I promised.

"It's far too revealing for someone your age," he frowned.

"I'm not a baby any more, Dad," I said.

"I think you look cool," said Lal, looking up from *Xena: Warrior Princess*.

"What do you think, Steve?" I asked.

He gave me a cursory glance up and down. "Not bad."

That's praise coming from him.

"You've done a really good job," said Mum, examining my stitching, "that silver brings out your blue eyes beautifully. Oh, let her wear it, Peter."

"Can't you sew some sleeves in?" said Dad, still not convinced.

"This is the look; it's not meant to have sleeves."

"Well, all right but make sure you keep your jacket on. And I'll pick you up at nine thirty. No later. I don't want you staying out late looking like that."

"Oh, Dad, please, ten at least. I'll be with Nesta and Izzie. They can stay out later. Please. *Pleeease*."

"Ten o'clock, no later," said Mum. "And Dad will be there waiting for you."

"And don't do anything I wouldn't," smirked Lal.

Permission from a fifteen-year-old to snog anyone, I thought.

I began to get ready in plenty of time. First I had a bath, but unluckily for me Steve and Lal had been in after their football practice. The soap was all slimy from where one of them had left it in a puddle of water in the soap dish, and the towels were on the floor and dripping wet. The joys of elder brothers. Not.

I went into Mum's room to get clean towels from the cupboard and that's when I noticed the jar. Wax for removing unwanted hair. Just the thing. I had a fuzz of hair growing under my arms and didn't want to get caught like that time the press saw Julia Roberts on her way to a film premiere. When she waved at them, they all photographed her hairy armpits. Not that the paparazzi are going to be at the Hollywood Bowl tonight but you never know who else might be. One day my prince will come.

Mum was out visiting next door so I snuck the jar into my room and read the instructions. Heat up, apply to the area, then pull off. Sounded simple enough so I went into the kitchen and warmed the wax up in a pan of water on the stove. I waited until it began to bubble.

"What you doing?" said Steve, coming in and sticking his nose in the pan. "Toffee?"

"Waxing," I said and showed him my underarms.

"Erlack," he said, backing away. "Girlie stuff."

"I'll do your chest if you like," I offered. His "chest hair" was a family joke. He has just the one. We all saw it in the garden this summer when he stripped off. We sang "macho macho macho man" to him. He was dead embarrassed.

"Won't it hurt?" he asked.

"Nah," I said. "It'll be easy. And so cheap. Izzie went for a leg wax last month and it cost her twelve quid. This is costing nothing."

Steve looked doubtful. Ben and Jerry looked up

from their sleeping spot under the table. Even they looked doubtful.

When the wax had cooled slightly, Jerry followed me upstairs and watched with interest as I took the spatula and smoothed it on liberally under both my arms.

Rip it off, in one firm upward motion, the packet directed.

I lifted my left arm, eased a bit of the now hard wax and began to tug.

Ohmigod. OHMIGOD. *Argggghhhhh!!!* Agony. My eyes began to water and my face flushed red. I tugged again. No way. Absolutely no way. It wouldn't come off. What was I going to do?

I took a deep breath and ripped. *ARGGGHH-HHHH!* I fell back on the bed, sweating in agony. Jerry immediately pounced up and gave my face a great wet lick.

Fending him off, I gasped, "Why does nobody tell you it's torture? Izzie never said."

Then I realized; I'd plastered the horrible stuff under both arms. But I couldn't go through that again. I just couldn't. But it would show if I didn't get it off. There was no way out.

I lay on the bed with my right arm above my head and timidly began to pull at the wax. The pain was indescribable. Jerry began to bark as I heard Mum come in through the front door.

"Mum," I called. "MuuUUM, I need you!"

I could hear her running up the stairs. "What is it?" she said, bursting through the door. "Has something happened?"

I nodded and pointed at my arm. "I used your wax to do my underarms."

Mum sat on the bed and started shaking with laughter. "Serves you right for snooping in my things," she said.

"I didn't want to do a Julia Roberts," I said.

Mum looked at me as though I was mad.

"It's not too bad when you use it on your legs," she said. "But your underarms," she started laughing again, "your poor underarms are a bit more sensitive."

"Have you got something that will dissolve it?" I asked hopefully.

She shook her head. "'Fraid not. Come on, let's get it over with. Arm up. Come ON. Arm up."

Tentatively I lifted my arm.

"Eyes closed, deep breath," said Mum.

I took a deep breath and she ripped.

"*ARGGGHHH!*" I screamed and Jerry howled in sympathy. It was like someone had sliced my skin off.

Mum leaned over and looked under my arm. "Bit of talc on there and no harm done." Then she grinned. "Welcome to the world of you have to suffer to be beautiful."

"Is she with you?" asked the ticket lady at the cinema.

Nesta nodded and tried to brave it out. "Three, please."

I turned away and tried to make myself disappear as everybody in the cinema queue stared at me.

"You do know that you have to be fifteen to see this film?"

Nesta nodded. "Yeah. Course."

"Do you have proof of your age?" said the lady, looking pointedly at me.

Nesta shook her head. "Not on me."

Izzie tugged Nesta's sleeve. "Come on, let's go."

As we made our way out of the foyer, I could hear the ticket lady tutting as she took money from the people next in line. "Honestly, kids these days," she said. "They're always trying it on."

I tried not to meet anyone's eyes as we snuck out. I felt awful. It was my fault. Izzie and Nesta could both easily pass for sixteen. It's me. Even though I've put some kohl on my eyes and am wearing lipstick. I've ruined their evening.

"Bad luck," said a voice from the queue.

We all turned back and saw Michael Brenman standing with a bunch of his mates waiting to get in. He was smiling at Nesta.

"Anyone can see the midget's underage," sneered Josie Riley, looking at me. She's a snotty Barbie lookalike from Year Eleven and well-known as a bully in our school, always picking on younger or smaller kids like me. She linked her arm through Michael's and pulled him away then looked back at us to say, "Stick to Disney in future, kids."

Nesta glared at her.

"What are you staring at?" said Josie.

"I'm just trying to visualise you with duct tape over your mouth," said Nesta.

I gulped. Ow. Move over Scary Spice, I thought.

Nesta Williams has come to town. I made for the exit. I didn't want any trouble. I knew what Josie could be like. Once she and her scabby mates had got me in the school loos and put my books in the sink and turned on the taps. Took me ages to get the pages dry.

Michael moved away from Josie and came up to Nesta. "You're new in school, aren't you?"

Nesta nodded, not taking her eyes from Josie who was still gobsmacked at her comment and was looking more than a bit unhappy. I don't think anyone had ever talked back to her before.

"We could get tickets for you," he said.

Izzie pulled Nesta's arm. "I don't think it's worth risking," she said to Michael. "If the ticket lady sees us going in, you'll only get in trouble as well."

"Come on, Mickie, leave the children to play," called Josie, moving up the queue. "It's almost our turn."

Michael turned back to the queue. "Well I'll see you around," he said and smiled again at Nesta.

"Wow!" said Nesta when we got outside. "Who is he? He's gorgeous, easily an eight out of ten."

"He's Michael Brenman, he goes to the sixth form college in Finchley," Izzie said.

"And he smelled amazing, lemony and clean, could you smell it?"

Actually I could. It had almost knocked me out. Never mind splash it on. He smelled as if he'd marinaded himself in it.

"Yes, er, lemony," I said diplomatically.

"What's he doing with that bullying creepoid? What's her name, anyway?" said Nesta.

"Josie Riley," I said. "Isn't she one of the girls who was calling you names that day at the bus stop?"

"Yeah. I wonder if she's his girlfriend" said Nesta.

"One of the many. I wouldn't bother if I were you," said Izzie. "Everybody fancies him."

"But he did smile at me and say I'll see you around. What do you think he meant?"

"I think he meant he'll see you around," said Izzie.

"Yeah but, see you around like I want to get to know you better? Or see you around, just see you around?" insisted Nesta.

"See you around, like join the list of girls I've already got gagging for me. He's cute and he knows it. Best play hard to get with someone like him."

"You reckon?" said Nesta, looking back at the cinema. "Mmm, very interesting."

She did look stunning tonight. Her hair was loose down her back and she was dressed in a denim jacket, tight jeans, and high-heeled ankle boots that made her legs look endless. It wasn't surprising that Michael had noticed her. All the boys were staring at her. She looks so sophisticated. Izzie looked good too in a tiny white cut-off top and combat jeans and trainers. I caught our reflections in the burger bar window. They both look like grown-ups who'd let their kid sister tag along.

"I'm really sorry," I said. "You'd have got in if it hadn't been for me."

"Don't be silly," said Izzie. "You look great tonight and I love your top. Where did you get it from?"

"I made it," I said. "Do you really like it?"

"It's fantastic," said Nesta, feeling the material. "I've got one just like it from Morgan. But mine's real silk."

Izzie saw my face drop. "But this is lovely," she said quickly. "It does look like real silk, Lucy."

"So what shall we do?" I said, trying to draw the

38

attention away from my top. "No point in going home now, and we're all being picked up from here later."

"Let's go and practice flirting," said Nesta, flicking her hair back as a group of lads walked past and looked appreciatively at her.

"Okay," I said, "but much good it'll do me. Boys never notice me even when I'm doing my best flirtie gertie act."

"Rubbish," said Izzie. "You're better with boys than anyone I know. Probably because you've got big brothers. Boys always find it easy to talk to you."

I winced when she said this as I remembered last summer. Izzie and I had been to watch Lal play football and we'd met this boy, and, for a change, he'd really chatted me up. I didn't really fancy him, but I was flattered by the attention. Then Izzie went off to get us some hot dogs, and he asked if I thought she liked him and would go on a date with him.

"Yeah, but only so as a way to get talking to you," I said. "Or Nesta. It's like I'm everyone's kid sister. One of the boys. They never take me seriously."

Suddenly I realized I sounded like a right saddo

so decided I'd make them laugh with my Madonna impersonation. My party piece at Christmas. It always makes Izzie crack up. I danced along behind them singing "Like a Virgin" at the top of my voice.

"Lucy," said Iz, giggling despite herself. "People are staring at you."

"It's one way to get noticed," I said. "Okay. Maybe not. So what shall we do, then?"

We looked around at the various alternatives.

"I suppose we could go bowling," said Nesta.

I felt my heart sink. Dad had given me my pocket money, but it was only enough for the movie, popcorn and a Coke. Bowling cost lots more and, of course, there'd be drinks.

"No point," said Izzie. "All the lanes will be booked on a Saturday night. Why don't we go and get some chips in the café and just hang out? They play good music over there." She pointed in the direction of one of the restaurants.

I sighed with relief. That would be okay, I thought. I could afford that.

"I feel rotten you didn't get in because of me," I whispered to Izzie as we made our way over.

"It's okay, honestly," she insisted. "I didn't really want to see the film that much anyway."

I knew she was trying to make me feel better. She'd been dying to see the film ever since it came out. Ewan McGregor was in it and he's one of Izzie's pin-ups.

On Sunday evening, I phoned Izzie to see if she wanted to come over and watch a video with Steve and Lal and me. Mum and Dad were going out, so we were going to get a couple of horrors in and scare ourselves stupid.

"Oh Izzie's not here," said Mrs Foster when I called. "She's gone to see that film. You know, the one with Ewan McGregor."

"Who's she gone with?" I asked, as though I couldn't guess.

"Nesta. She called for her half an hour ago. Er . . . are you not going with them?"

No. I wasn't going with them. And I know exactly why I hadn't been asked.

Chapter 4

Love
at
First Sight

School was awful. I was avoiding Izzie and Nesta. I'd been really hurt last night. But I'd got the message. Izzie'd moved on and didn't want me around any more.

I ignored them both in English though I could see Izzie was trying to catch my eye. I kept my head down and pretended I was fascinated by Shakespeare's sonnets.

Mr. Johnson was substituting the class, and I usually like his lessons. He's big and jolly with a red

---

Chapter 4

Love
at
First Sight

School was awful. I was avoiding Izzie and Nesta. I'd been really hurt last night. But I'd got the message. Izzie'd moved on and didn't want me around any more.

I ignored them both in English though I could see Izzie was trying to catch my eye. I kept my head down and pretended I was fascinated by Shakespeare's sonnets.

Mr. Johnson was substituting the class, and I usually like his lessons. He's big and jolly with a red

42

beard like a Viking. He chalked a load of stuff up on the board then said, "Now, watch the blackboard while I go through it."

Everyone cracked up and when he realized what he'd said, he started laughing as well. But not me. Me and Hamlet. We got things to think about. "To be friends with Iz and Nesta or not to be? That is the question."

After English, we had a special lesson with Mrs. Allen all about third world countries and their need for help. Mrs. Allen is our headmistress so everyone was on their best behavior and really quiet. But it wasn't just because she was taking the class. It was depressing hearing about the hunger and wars in some areas.

We had to get into groups to discuss the lesson so I made sure I was in Mo Harrison and Candice Carter's group so I didn't have to speak to Izzie or Nesta.

"I don't understand why people fight," I said, feeling guilty that I was having my own conflict with Izzie, "and over something stupid like land. I reckon it's like, if you look at the sky there aren't any fences or boundaries. It should be the same on the ground."

"Yeah," said Mo. "Why can't we all just share everything?"

"Same sun, same air, same earth," I said. "It hardly makes sense that there's famine in the world when you see all the shops with food spilling out the doors. And people over here on diets all the time when on the other side of the world, other people haven't even got enough to eat."

The lesson made me feel very sad. I mean, Mum's been going on about poor people and the starving for years. Like when one of us wouldn't eat dinner or something. But I never took much notice. Watching the slides Mrs. Allen showed and seeing the real people was different. I could see it made us all think. I'd got all freaked out about not having a best friend any more but in some places, some people have just lost their parents or their kids.

I don't know what to do about Izzie and Nesta. It seems so petty to fall out, especially after today's lesson. I feel really confused now and don't know what to think.

Maybe I could go and be a volunteer in the third world when I grow up. But then what could I volunteer to do? My only special talent is making cheese omelettes, so it's probably best I learn a skill first. But what?

At lunchtime, I was out of class before Nesta and Izzie could catch up and made my way to the library. I needed time to think and decided I'd go and look through books about courses and careers and stuff and see if there was anything I fancied or might be good at.

It all seemed a bit daunting as I leafed through the pages; there's so much to choose from.

"Hey, Luce," said Izzie, coming up behind where I was sitting at a desk. "What're you doing in here? Me and Nesta have been looking every-where for you."

I pointed at the books. "Trying to decide on my brilliant career."

I carried on reading as if she wasn't there, but the silence felt uncomfortable and the words were swimming on the page in front of me.

"You've been very quiet lately, Luce. Is everything okay?"

I felt as if I'd swallowed a wad of chewing gum and it had got stuck in my throat.

"Luce?"

"How was the film?" I finally said.

Izzie looked embarrassed. "I know. Mum said you called." She slid into the chair next to mine. "Nesta's got drama tonight so why don't you come back to mine? Just us. We'll have a laugh. Tell you what, I'll do your birth chart. I've found this fab site on the Net and we'll see what the future holds."

It did sound tempting, but I didn't say anything. I still felt confused and pushed out.

"Oh pleeease, Lucy. We could do the Tarot cards as well. It might help you get some more ideas about what you want to do."

"I promised I'd help Dad do his shopping at the wholesaler's," I lied.

"You could come after. It won't take long with your dad. Look. I'm sorry about last night. I suppose I didn't think. Nesta was on her own and the wicked stepsisters were visiting round at ours. I had to get out. I knew you'd be okay. At least you've got a nor-mal family."

I had to laugh at that. "Normal? Us? What planet are you on?"

I have to say I know what she means though. Her set-up is pretty complicated.

1 Her mum and dad got divorced about seven years ago, when Izzie was little, then her mum remarried.

2 Her stepdad's a lot older than Izzie's mum and he has two grown-up daughters from his first marriage, both accountants like their father. Izzie calls them the wicked stepsisters.

3 Oh. And her dad remarried as well. He married someone a lot younger. Anna. At least Izzie likes her.

She had a little boy, Tom, who's two now, and Izzie completely dotes on him.

So, see what I mean? Stepsisters, a stepdad, and a stepmum *and* a stepbrother, as well as her real mum and dad.

Pretty complicated.

Izzie wasn't giving up on me. "Oh, please come over, we haven't had time on our own for ages."

Understatement, I thought, but I couldn't stay mad at her. We've been friends for too long and I don't want to lose her.

"Okay," I said, realizing that now I was going to

have to help Dad. "After I've finished with Dad, I'll get him to drop me off at yours."

It was on the way to Izzie's that I saw Him. We were driving through Highgate past St. Michael's school, and he was coming out of the gates with another boy. We were stuck in traffic coming up to the roundabout and as the car slowed down, he darted across in front of us. A ten-out-of-ten, a face like Leonardo DiCaprio's, but he was taller with olive skin and dark hair. Absolutely drop dead goooorgeousissimo.

I watched him walk away down the pavement on the other side. It was like time stood still, and suddenly I understood what all the fuss is about. Usually I never see boys I like. Not really. Even at Hollywood Bowl, I've never seen anyone who's caught my eye. Not like him. I wonder if he goes there to the movies? I wonder who he is? I must find out. I'll persuade Izzie to come up to Highgate and hang out. There are loads of cafés there. He must go into one of them sometimes after school, all the St. Michael's boys do. My heart was racing.

It had happened. At last. Love at first sight.

As we drove on, I felt elated. I had a goal: Meet that boy.

Izzie lives a few roads away from me on the Finchley borders. Their house is one of those mock Tudor jobs, detached, with gardens at the front and back. It's very neat inside and so quiet compared to the bedlam at ours. The kitchen looks like an operating theater, all white and steel. I always feel I have to talk quietly even when there's no one there.

Izzie's mum likes things just so. Izzie says it's because she's a Virgo and they're perfectionists. Even though they have a cleaner come every day, Mrs. Foster still likes to clear around us if we're there. I'm a bit scared of her—like once I was eating an apple in the hall when I was waiting for Iz.

"Where are you going with that apple?" she said, coming up behind me.

"Er, nowhere," I said.

"Well, don't drop bits on my clean carpet, will you?"

And she went into the kitchen and brought me out a knife and a plate. Eek. She wouldn't last ten minutes in our house.

I'm glad she's not back tonight so Iz and I have the place to ourselves. Izzie's room is different from the rest of the house. It's the only room that has any color as Mrs. Foster favors neutral shades, on the carpets, curtains, and walls. And she only wears black. Black with pearls. Always immaculate and expensive-looking. Her dark hair cut into a severe bob to match her personality.

Izzie painted her room herself and she's done it a deep turquoise. "A very healing color," she told me. And she's got purple curtains and cushions. It looks vibrant and interesting. Like Izzie.

She lit one of her nice smelly candles then cranked up the computer. I looked at her posters. Ewan, of course, Suzanne Vega, who's one of Izzie's heroines, and a dolphin. Izzie's big on them. She wants to go swimming with them one day. Honestly, she's more like my mum than I am.

I flopped on the bed, and Izzie sat at her desk and starting pressing keys.

"Right, I've been dying to try this. I got some new software and it works out a personalized horoscope for you," she said. "You were born May twenty-fourth, Gemini, right? What time?"

"Five past midnight," I said. I remember because it's Dad's birthday as well and Mum says I was his birthday present. Only just made it by five minutes though.

Izzie punched in the information. "Give it a few minutes and it will tell us all about you. While we're waiting for it, we'll do the Tarot cards."

She gave me the pack and I started shuffling.

"Have you done your chart yet?" I said.

"Yep," grinned Izzie. "Aquarius, sign of the genius, humanitarian, eccentric . . ."

"Barking mad, you mean," I said. "And I dunno about the genius bit, but the rest sounds like you. I suppose you are humanitarian most of the time when you're not swanning off to see films without me."

Izzie threw a pillow at me. She knew I was teasing.

"What did you think of that lesson with Mrs. Allen?" I asked. "Sad, wasn't it?"

Izzie nodded. "I'm going to write a song about it."

"Why?" I asked. "It's a bit of a depressing subject for people to listen to."

"Ah, but songwriters have as much power, if not more than some politicians."

"How can they?" I laughed. She was always coming out with mad stuff like this.

"Well look at Bob Geldoff. He did loads, didn't he, when he did that Band Aid concert? Raised more money than anyone in years. And look at Comic Relief. Millions in a night. And John Lennon. 'All we are saying is give peace a chance.' I reckon if you can write a song or a book or make a film, sometimes you can touch more people that way than boring politicians droning on. Music makes people think. They listen to lyrics. Better than lecturing them or dropping a leaflet through the door that only gets put in the wastepaper bin."

This is one of the things I like best about Izzie. She makes *me* think. She's so wise. Mum says Izzie's an old soul. When I asked if I was, Mum looked at me strangely and said, "No, love, I think it's your first time on the planet." I don't know if that was a compliment or an insult.

And Izzie's right. I'd only thought about being a volunteer and going wherever needed and doing some cooking or clearing up or something. But if you could reach people and touch them, there'd be more people to help. If only I had a skill like she has with her songwriting.

"I was talking to Nesta about it at break," continued Iz. "She wasn't into going and being a volunteer and sleeping in a tent and having no MTV. She says her plan is to be mega mega rich when she's a model then she can give some of her money away."

"What, Nesta? I wouldn't have thought she ever thought about anybody but herself."

"You've got to give her a chance, Lucy, she's okay. And I think it's a good plan. I mean, you could give your time and be a volunteer, or you could become mega rich like Nesta wants to be and give your money instead and pay to train volunteers. You know, actually do something with your money as well as having a good time with it. Best of both worlds."

"I guess," I said. I didn't want to admit that Nesta's idea was pretty smart. Nesta. Nesta. Nesta.

"Finished shuffling?"

I nodded, and she took the pack, sat on the floor, and split the cards into three piles. Then she consulted her book.

"This is a Grand Cross," she said, laying the cards out. "It tells you the Past, the Present, and the Future."

I flopped on the beanbag next to her. I felt

happy. Iz and me. Me and Iz talking about stuff, and Iz predicting my future.

"What does it say, Madam Rose?"

"Oh, interesting," Iz murmured. "Very interesting. The card that crosses you is the Wheel of Fortune. It signifies a new chapter. A turning point."

"Tell me about it," I said. "Decisions, decisions, decisions."

"The influence passing over you is the High Priestess. She indicates potential unfulfilled, but it will be revealed."

"Oh, I hope so," I said. "It's been awful lately with everyone knowing what they want to do but me." I pointed to the next card. "This looks *très* interesting."

"The Lovers. In your future, it indicates a love affair."

"Oh, fantastic. . . ." I was dying to tell her about the boy I'd seen.

"But there's some kind of trial or choice involved. Lucy, why are you blushing? You've gone scarlet."

"Izzie," I couldn't hold it in any longer. "I've seen someone. . . ."

"Someone?"

"A boy. I think he goes to St. Michael's. . . ."

Izzie grinned. "And . . . ?"

"Well I've only just seen him. When I was driving here with Dad. He was coming out of the school gates and was absolutely gorgeous. Could that be what the Lovers means? Maybe I'm going to meet him. Does it say anything about him?"

Izzie looked at the card spread. "Maybe. Here. There's the Page of Swords card in your future. That could be him."

I looked at the card, a young man with a sword held high.

"That *must* be him. Who else could it be? It's amazing. He's so gorgeous. I thought maybe we could hang out in Highgate after school one day . . ."

"Well if it's in the cards, you'll meet him anyway." Izzie looked concerned as she read her book. "But he could be ruthless. The Page of Swords is sometimes deceitful. Not to be trusted. So go carefully, Lucy. You don't even know what he's like yet."

Nothing could dampen my enthusiasm. "Oh, I could see he's not like that. He had a really nice face."

Izzie continued looking at the cards. "Well let's see what the outcome is."

"I don't like the look of the last card," I said.

It had a picture of a tower on fire with a body falling out of the window.

"Oh, that's the Tower," said Izzie. "I know it looks a bit scary, but actually it's a good card to get. It represents the influences around you and means in order to move forward, old ways must be broken down, but in their place comes greater freedom. See, the card after it is the World, the outcome of the reading. That's a fantastic card to get. It means happiness, strength, and success. The realization of a goal. Wow. Lucy, this is a really positive reading. I mean, it says there will be a bit of confrontation, change, and adjustment, but the outcome is very good."

I left Izzie's that night feeling on top of the world. Even my personalized horoscope was good. And she was going to do one for Nesta as well. Astrology's one of Izzie's career choices. She might do it as well as being a songwriter. Lucky thing. It must be great, having not only one idea of what you want to be, but two. And I still haven't decided on anything. Still, when Izzie printed my horoscope, it said pretty much the same as the cards. It was all going to be all right. Break down to break through, it said. It was all a process. I was going through a time of change and mustn't resist. The outcome was good.

Things were looking up. It was going to be okay. Success. Achievement. Me and Izzie were all right with each other again. But best of all, the Page of Swords. I couldn't wait to meet him.

Horoscopes

Lucy: May 24th. Gemini. Cancer rising. Moon in Taurus.

Saturn the taskmaster is forcing you to look deeper into your goals. It's only by experiencing testing circumstances that we learn where our destiny lies. Don't resist.

With Neptune and Venus so close, romance is in the air, but tread warily as things may not be as they appear.

Nesta: August 18th. Leo. Aries rising. Moon in Gemini.

Mercury is moving retrograde at the moment so causing you to misread signals. Misunderstandings are likely to occur. Around the New Moon, you're more positive and productive as new opportunities present themselves.

Izzie: January 26th. Aquarius. Gemini rising. Moon in Scorpio.

The relationship between the Sun and Neptune means that you may misjudge a situation which needs careful handling. Don't be surprised if people overreact. Close relationships may be tense until this phase is over.

Chapter 5

Disaster
Strikes

I don't believe it. I just don't believe it. What started out as a brilliant week has just ended in complete, total, and utter disaster.

Course Izzie told Nesta I'd seen someone I liked. That part was okay, in fact Nesta was really enthusiastic, though I did feel a prat when I had to admit that I hadn't even spoken to him.

"So how do you know what he's like?" she said.

"I don't. I just know we'll get on," I replied.

"Then first of all, we have to get him to notice you," she said.

"I know," I replied.

I'd been thinking about it a lot. Is he going to be another in a long line of people who think I'm twelve and don't even register me? No. I was being positive. I'd find a way.

Don't wait for your ship to come in, swim out to it.

I had a plan.

Luckily I had Izzie to myself for the week. Nesta's in the school play and has rehearsals every night, and, I have to say, I was relieved. Not wanting to be mean or anything, but she's what Lal calls a Top Babe, and the chances were if He saw her, I wouldn't even get a look-at.

So. The plan was that Izzie and I'd get the bus up to Highgate and hopefully bump into him, sort of accidentally on purpose.

Tuesday P.M.: went to Highgate. I like it up there. Tall, white Georgian houses set back behind wrought iron railings around the square. *Très* posh. And the village isn't like the rest of London with big supermarkets and chain stores. The shops up there are all individual and interesting. Little jewelery shops and nick-nacky places. We got so absorbed in looking in the windows at first that we almost forgot to look for Mr. MC. Mystery Contestant. (That's Izzie's nickname for him.)

We tore ourselves away from the shops and walked past the school about twenty times. We hung around at the bus stop. Boys of every shape and size were pouring out. But did He appear? No.

Wednesday P.M.: Highgate. This time we went to the cafés. Café Uno. Café Rouge. Costa's. I was getting cappuccinoed out by the time we'd finished. Everywhere was full of St. Michael's boys. But Mr. Top Totty? (My nickname for him.) No.

"Maybe he's off with flu or something," said Izzie.

"Maybe I imagined him," I said. His image was already starting to fade in my mind.

Thursday P.M.: Walked past the school *and* did the cafés. I was running out of pocket money. It's an expensive business looking for the Mystery Contestant. Still no show.

Friday: Izzie was convinced he's off with a bug.

"But you don't know for definite," I said. "And if he was, he might be better by now."

We did our usual walk past the school, but, once again, he didn't appear.

"Let's go to Costa's," said Izzie. "That's where most of them go."

Just at that moment, we saw Nesta crossing the road and waving. She looked amazing. Although we don't have to wear school uniform, she sometimes wears her own version and puts on a shirt, tie, skirt, and three-quarter stockings. Very Britney Spears. She'd hitched her skirt up and her legs looked fantastic. Cars were almost driving into lampposts as male drivers did double-takes.

"Rehearsal was canceled so I thought I'd come and join the boy-chasing troops," she grinned.

My heart sank as Izzie told her our plan and we set off for Costa's.

"I'll meet you in there," she said, "I'm just going to get a copy of *Bliss*. There's a piece in there on the Clothes Show I want to read."

Izzie and I went to the café and settled ourselves at a table by the window so we could look out as well as in. I did a quick check of the customers. No, he wasn't there.

That's when my brilliant plan took on a life of its own.

Izzie went to get the cappuccinos and I looked out at the passersby.

Suddenly my mouth dropped open. Nesta was coming out of the shop and down the road. And guess who she was with? Him. MC. Two minutes in the shop and she'd got talking to him. Talk about fast worker. He was even laughing at something she said. I *knew* this would happen if Nesta came along.

Oh no. Even worse, she was coming over the road. With him. Coming into the café. She couldn't possibly know that he was my He and I decided not to let on. But I felt myself going red and prayed no one would notice.

She burst in with him in tow and came up to us just as Izzie came back with the coffees.

"Iz, Lucy. This is Tony," she said.

Close up he was even better-looking than I remembered. Sleepy brown velvet eyes, thick black eyelashes, and a gorgeous mouth with a full bottom lip.

"Tony's my brother," said Nesta.

My jaw dropped and Nesta started laughing.

"I know what you're thinking," she said. "How can that be?"

I was thinking exactly that. I mean, Nesta's half Jamaican. Skin like coffee ice cream. Tony's complexion is more Mediterranean. Luckily no one had noticed my face which by this time was bright scarlet. Everyone was too busy looking at Tony.

"He's my half brother," she explained. "My mum is his dad's second wife. A year after he married my mum they had me. So same dad, different mums."

She'd told us she had a brother, but I didn't expect this! No wonder she and Izzie have so much in common. But *brother*. He's Nesta's brother. Half, step, or whatever. Oh NO. Now I can never tell anyone, not Izzie, not Nesta. With Nesta's big mouth, she's bound to blab to him that I fancy him and have been up here looking for him. I'd end up looking really desperate. Can life possibly get any worse?

"Hi," he smiled at us. "Which one of you is Lucy?"

I felt all wobbly and faint when he looked at me.

"I am," I said weakly and blushing even more furiously.

"Nesta tells me you've got your eye on one of the St. Michael's kids. I go there so I might know him. What year is he in? What does he look like?"

"Er, tall, er . . . hair," I stuttered, trying my best not to describe the vision standing in front of me. "He was too far away for me to get a really close look."

Izzie and Nesta cracked up laughing.

"Gorgeous, apparently," said Izzie, coming to my rescue. "We know that much at least. Just find us the best-looking boy at your school. He'll do."

"Well you're looking at him," boasted Tony. "But I'll try and look out for the next best thing."

"Big-head," said Nesta.

I wanted to die.

Thankfully Tony didn't stay around too long, and after a while I got up to go as well. I wanted to run away and hide.

All the St. Michael's boys were oggling Nesta and one even sent her over a coffee and a Danish. Izzie got chatting to some strange-looking boy with long hair in the corner who was reading *Mojo* magazine. She went over to him and soon they were busy discussing music and the charts. I felt like a spare part. No one noticed me. It's like I'm invisible. It's weird: When I feel good, I can make people laugh, but when I'm down, I disappear. And Tony's gone home. Not only is he Nesta's brother, but he was right about him being the best-looking boy at the school. I can't believe Izzie didn't clock that he was the One.

"I'm off," I said.

"Don't you want to stay and see if Mr. Right appears?" said Nesta, spooning the froth from her cappuccino. "See I reckon the reason you haven't seen him is that he's been doing some class after school. They do all sorts of extra curricular stuff—fencing, music, drama. Tony told me. He's often late because he's been doing something or other. Hang around another half hour or so and another lot of guys will be out."

How could I tell her that He *was* out? That *He* was Tony. Tony, who was now, thanks to Big Gob Nesta, only too happy to help me find my mystery boy.

I didn't want her to suspect so I sat down again and went along with the pretence that I was still looking for Mr. Right. Luckily Nesta changed the subject. She's too excited about the up-and-coming Clothes Show to think about anything else at the moment.

"Premier, Storm, and Select are all sending talent scouts to the show," she read from her magazine, "and both Erin O'Connor and Vernon were discovered at shows in the past. And we could get a makeover. There will be people there giving a whole new look."

Izzie came back to sit with us, and her and Nesta spent the next half hour gabbing about what they were going to wear and what they were going to do there. Makeovers, accessories, manicures.

"What are you going to wear, Lucy?" asked Nesta.

"I haven't thought about it," I said. I'd been miles away, thinking about Tony. I had a million questions I wanted to ask Nesta.

What birth sign is he? Izzie could do his chart to see if we were a good match.

What does he like doing?

What sort of girls does he like?

What did Nesta and Izzie think he thought of

me? He had smiled at me very warmly.

And why doesn't he live with his mum? Usually when a couple split up, the children stay with their mum. So how come Tony lives with his dad but Nesta's mum? Where's his mum?

And oh! Worst of all. What if *Izzie* fancies Tony? She's bound to. He's so cute. Irresistible. *Magnifique*. How can I find out without her guessing that he's the MC?

But I couldn't ask anything. It had to be my secret.

That ship I was going to swim out to? I think it just sunk.

Chapter 6

The New Me

Izzie's just phoned. Apparently Tony told Nesta he thought I was a sweet kid. What kind of word is that? Sweet? It's like being told you're nice. Pleasant. Agreeable. *Urggghhh*.

What makes me "me"? I'm sweet. Yuk.

I don't want to be sweet. I want to be a Babe. A Boy Magnet.

But no. I'm *sweet*.

Sweeeeet. A sweet kid. Kid.

But at least he noticed me. And said something to Nesta.

I look at myself in the bedroom mirror. I suppose I do look kind of sweet. Small, flat-chested, not the slightest evidence of a bust. And that's another thing. Izzie and Nesta both have breasts, in fact Izzie says hers have taken on a life of their own lately. But me, nothing. Pinpricks. Pimples. I have the body of a nine-year-old boy.

I could have my hair cut. It's been long for years. I could have it done spiky. And highlighted. Although it's blond, I could have white blond streaked through it. Yeah, I thought. Like how? On my pocket money?

I look around my bedroom. It was last painted when I was ten. Pink. The beginning of my pink phase. And fluffy toys everywhere, on the window ledge, the wardrobe, the bed. I picked up Mr. Mackety, my favorite teddy. He's fat and grumpy-looking and I've had him since I was five. I thought about chucking him out. Nope. Mr. Mackety in a bin liner? Too awful. No way. Can't. We've been through too much together. Still, I can't deny the overall effect of my room is sweet. Sweeeeet.

I went downstairs to see what everyone was

doing, but the house was quiet for a change. Mum was out doing her Saturday shopping, Dad was at the health shop, and the boys were out at football.

I spied Mum's Angel Cards in a bowl on the kitchen table. I took the pack and shuffled them.

"Okay, oh clever clogs cards, let's see what words of wisdom you have for me today." I picked a card and read.

"*'The people who get on in the world are the people who get up and look for the circumstances they want. And if they can't find them, make them.' George Bernard Shaw.*"

Well, that's telling me! If they can't find them, make them.

Okay. I will, Mr. Shaw. I'll do my own makeover. I've had enough of mooching about feeling miserable. Feeling like second best. I'm not like that normally. It's only lately I've been feeling peculiar. But I'm going to fight back. I'll show them all who's a sweet kid.

I sat at the table and made a list of all the changes I want to make.

1 My hair.
2 My bedroom.

3 My clothes.

4 My life.

Mum came in the back door laden with bags of groceries.

"What're you doing?" she asked.

"Changing," I said, then read her my Angel Card.

"But you're lovely the way you are," she said and hugged me. "My lovely sweet Lucy."

Arggggghhhh. That word again.

"I don't want to be sweet anymore."

"Well what do you want to be?"

"I don't knOWWWW."

Mum sat down and looked at me with concern. "Are you happy, Lucy? That's the main thing."

"Yes. No. Sort of. Sometimes."

Mum laughed, then saw my paper with the list.

"Things I want to change," I said.

"Oh but not your hair, your lovely hair!" She read down the list. "Tell you what, though. You can decorate your bedroom if you like. It's needed doing for a while now."

"Really? Can I?"

"Pick some paint colors and the boys can give you a hand painting. Then we'll look in the

Curtain Exchange for curtains. They won't be new, but they have a great selection there and we're bound to find something you like. Or we could go to the market and get some fabric and make them ourselves."

Fantastic. It's a start.

Then I looked at the patchwork of colors on the wall opposite me. "But, Mum, what about the kitchen? You've been wanting to do that for ages."

"Oh, that can wait," she said. "I've got used to it in a funny sort of way. No. It's decided. Lucy gets a new bedroom."

I couldn't wait to get started. "I'll call Izzie and she can help me choose colors," I said. "If you can't find the circumstances you want, make them. I like that."

I ran into the hallway to phone Iz.

"Don't try to change everything in one go!" called Mum. "Remember, he who would climb the ladder must begin at the bottom."

I stuck my head back round the door. "I know. And Rome wasn't built in a day. See, Mum, you're not the only one round here who knows quotes. By the way, where did all that Oxfam stuff go?"

"Back in the cupboard under the stairs. Why? What are you up to?"

"This is the new me. I'm going to make myself some new gear. Just you wait. That halter neck top was just the beginning.'"

Mum laughed as I ran off to the phone.

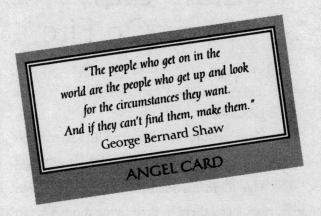

"The people who get on in the world are the people who get up and look for the circumstances they want. And if they can't find them, make them."
George Bernard Shaw

ANGEL CARD

Chapter 7

Liar, Liar,
Pants On Fire

"Let's go over to Nesta's this afternoon," said Izzie. "Her mum has loads of fab interior design magazines. I saw them in their living room. We can browse through . . . Lucy, Lucy? Are you there?"

"Yes, yes, I'm here," I said. "Sorry. I dropped the phone."

Ohmigod. Nesta's. I know I've got to go some time, now that we seem to be officially a three-some. But Nesta's? What if Tony's there? Part of me is dying to see him again. Part of me is dreading it. What if Nesta and Izzie suss me out? I'm bound to go pink if he's there and I never was much good at hiding anything from Iz. But then again, he might not be there. Either way, I can find out a bit more about him. Oh decisions, decisions, decisions.

"Izzie?" I said seriously.

"Yes, Lucy?" she said seriously then laughed.

"Do you fancy Tony?"

"God no. Not my type at all. Too pretty pretty boy. And he's a bit too sure of himself, you know what I mean?"

"Yeah," I sighed with relief.

"Why, do you fancy him?" she asked.

"Course not," I lied. "Too pretty pretty boy."

Liar, liar, pants on fire, said a voice in my head.

"So, shall we go over to Nesta's?" Izzie asked again.

"Okay," I said. "I'll come to your house later and we can go together." Eek. Er. The new brave me. If I plaster on a load of foundation, perhaps no one'll notice if I blush.

Nesta's flat is amazing. She lives on the ground floor of a detached Victorian property near Highgate. One of those places you hear estate agents describe as having character and original features. Lovely old cornicing in the hallway and stained-glass windows.

"Are you okay, Lucy?" Nesta asked, taking our coats. "You're looking a bit pale."

"Oh, I'm fine," I said, immediately reddening under my matte factor 16. "I like your flat."

"Wait until you see the rest of it," Nesta said proudly. "I'll give you the tour. You've already seen it, Izzie, so make yourself at home."

She led us into a large room with French windows at the back. It looked warm and welcoming with deep red walls and curtains and plush brown velvet sofas. The overall look was a mix of Eastern and old, stylish, and comfortable.

Izzie helped herself to a pile of magazines by the fireplace and flopped down on a sofa while Nesta led me into a country style kitchen-diner at the side.

"It's huge in here," I said, staring around. "You don't often find flats this big."

"I know," said Nesta. "Dad likes the big old rooms with high ceilings, and the houses like that were out of his price range. He says we were lucky to find a flat like this with three bedrooms."

She led me out of the kitchen and down the corridor and opened a door. "Mum and Dad's room."

I peeked in. "Are they here?"

"No," said Nesta. "Dad's in America and Mum's on late shift."

"Nice," I said as I looked at their bedroom. A big square room done in honey golds with soft muslin at a bay window overlooking the garden.

Back out in the corridor hung black and white photographs of bleak landscapes—mountains and sea against dramatic skies, each one beautifully framed.

"Who took these?" I asked. "They're great."

"Dad. It's one of his hobbies," said Nesta, opening the next door. "Tony's room."

I trooped in after her feeling like I was spying. The room was done in grays and blues and he was very tidy for a boy. His books and papers were neatly stacked on his computer desk. Steve and Lal's rooms always look like a bomb has hit them. Then I saw the posters on his wall. Jennifer Lopez. The Corrs. Buffy the Vampire Slayer.

"Tony likes girls," laughed Nesta when she saw me staring.

"Did your mum decorate?" I asked.

Nesta nodded. "She did an interior design course before she was a newsreader. Says it's always good to have something to fall back on. She reckons you have a limited time working as a presenter on television. They keep hiring younger and younger presenters and she says oldies like her can get thrown on the scrap heap at any time."

"You're so lucky to live somewhere like this," I said. I was really impressed. "She's got a great eye for color, your mum."

"You've got a good eye as well, Lucy," said Nesta. "You always dress in colors that suit you and that halter neck you made was fabulous."

I felt really chuffed. That was the nicest thing Nesta had ever said to me. I suddenly warmed to her and decided it would be all right to ask the question I'd been dying to ask ever since I met Tony. Where is his mum?

Just as I plucked up the courage, we heard the front door open. My heart began to race. Oh, please don't let it be him. Please don't let it be him and he find me standing in his bedroom.

We heard footsteps coming down the corridor

and a moment later, Tony appeared. He looked startled to see us.

"Just giving Lucy the tour," said Nesta.

Tony grinned. "Only too happy to come home to find a pretty girl in my bedroom. Hi, Lucy."

He remembered my name. Oh, God. And he gets better-looking every time I see him.

"Hi." I could feel myself going puce and prayed my makeup was doing its job.

"So how's the search for the mystery man going?" he asked. "The one with the, er . . . hair."

"Er . . . I haven't seen him again . . ." I muttered.

"He'll turn up," said Nesta. "But we need a plan. To get Lucy noticed. You like girls, Tone. What do you look for? What do you find attractive?"

Tony looked deep into my eyes as he thought about his answer. "First I like girls who are funny. Who can make me laugh. And girls who know who they are," he said finally, "you know, who know what they want and where they're going. Confidence, I suppose. It's a real turn-on."

Girls who know who they are. Confidence. That's the last thing I needed to hear. I glanced over at Nesta, hoping she'd shut up or change the subject or something, and I could swear she was laughing. I bet she's guessed that it's Tony I like and she's told him. He's probably having a laugh as well.

Izzie came in to join us and the three of them spent ages blabbing on about how to get noticed by boys. I felt like I'd frozen inside.

Suddenly I wanted to go home. To our mismatched walls and my baby pink bedroom. And my mum.

Tips for getting noticed
by the opposite sex

Nesta's

- › Be blindingly beautiful. There's no such thing as a plain girl, only one who can't be bothered. Lipstick, sunglasses and anyone can be a Babe.
- › Wear heels to make your legs look longer.
- › Get a Wonderbra.
- › Always have clean shiny hair.
- › Stand up straight. Don't slouch. It's the first thing they teach at model school. Good posture makes you look more confident and makes your body look slimmer.

Izzie's

- Relax. Boys hate clingy or desperate.
- Make eye contact, then smile.
- Find out his interests then ask him about them.
- Laugh at his jokes.
- Don't be too available. Play hard to get for a while as boys like a challenge.

Tony's

- Be confident. Don't carry on about what you don't like about yourself.
- Look fit. Boys respond when they like what they see.
- Flirt outrageously, then go home, it will leave him wanting more.
- Don't smoke. It makes your breath stink as well as your clothes and hair.

Lucy's

- Pray for a miracle.
- Grow another six inches.

Chapter 8

Giving Nesta a Second Chance

"I'm sure she wouldn't do anything like that," said Mum after I'd blurted out all my worst fears about Tony when I got home later that day. "Nesta seems like a really nice girl."

Mums are a peculiar species. Sympathetic when you don't expect it and unsupportive when you do.

"She was laughing at me, Mum, I swear she was. And she kept asking him what he liked about girls. Then Izzie joined in. And they were all going on about how to get a boy. It was so embarrassing."

"So you really like this Tony, do you?"

I nodded, turning my usual bright purple.

"How old is he?"

"Seventeen," I said.

"Well, if he's got any sense at all, he'll like you too."

"Yeah but it's like, I'm Nesta's friend. His kid sister's friend. How am I ever going to get him to take me seriously?"

Suddenly I felt awkward talking about it all to Mum. I should be discussing this with Izzie. But that was out of the question.

"You won't ever say, will you, Mum? You know, that I like Tony. Not to anyone. Not Steve or Lal or Nesta or Izzie or anyone."

"Course not if you don't want me to. But I don't really understand why Nesta and Izzie can't know. They are your friends."

I pulled a face.

"Why the face?" asked Mum.

I shrugged. "Since Nesta came, it's like her and Izzie are friends and I'm the odd one out."

"And how do you feel about that?" she asked, going into shrink mode. I felt like one of her patients. I've heard her come out with the "and how do you feel?" line a hundred times when she's been on the phone to one of them.

"I *feel* left out," I said.

"I'm sure you're imagining it," said Mum. "Izzie will always be your friend. And I think Nesta wants to be too if you'll let her."

"You don't understand," I said.

I felt cross. How could she know what it had been like lately?

I wasn't going to say any more.

"Well how do you think Nesta feels?" asked Mum. "It can't have been easy for her, starting a new school, new area, and everything."

"Oh, she's fine. Her life is completely together. She lives in an amazing flat. All the boys fancy her. And now she has Izzie."

I felt as if I was going to cry. Everyone cared more about Nesta Williams than they did about me. I bit my bottom lip. I wasn't going to blub. Not in front of Mum. No one understands. And Tony likes girls who know who they are and what they want, and I still don't have a clue. And there's no one to talk to anymore.

I picked up Mum's *Good Housekeeping* magazine and started leafing through it. She got the message. Counseling session over.

She started tidying up around me, and as she moved things off the kitchen table, she put her hand on her cards.

"Angel Card?" she asked with a grin. Now even *she* was laughing at me. It wasn't funny.

"No thanks," I grumbled. "Those stupid cards have got me into enough trouble as it is."

"Suit yourself," said Mum and went upstairs.

When she'd gone, I noticed she'd left the cards on the table. I stuck my tongue out at them. But then I couldn't resist. Just one more to see what it said. I picked them up, shuffled and chose one.

If you want a friend, be a friend, it said.

Argggghhhh. I threw the card down. This was getting spooky. They always seemed to say just the right thing. If you want a friend, be a friend. That was it. I hadn't exactly gone out of my way to be Nesta's friend. I'd been so busy thinking that she'd stolen Izzie from me that I hadn't even thought about how I'd come across to her.

And I suppose Mum was right. It can't have

been easy for her starting a new school where everyone already knows each other.

Okay, Nesta Williams, I thought. One more chance. I will be a friend to you.

And see what happens.

I went up to my room and had a good think about what I could do to be more of a friend to Nesta.

Make her a cake. No, that's silly. Anyway she's always on a diet.

Invite her over for a video night with Steve and Lal. No. Lal will only drool over her.

I know. I'll organize a girlie night. Izzie and I often have them, well used to have them, we haven't done one for ages. We can put on face masks and do manicures and do each other's hair. Nesta'll like that with the Clothes Show coming up. And I'll be really really nice. In fact, I'll even be sweet, seeing as I seem to be so good at it.

I looked into my purse to see how much money I had left then popped out to the local chemist so I had everything in.

I got an avocado face mask, some purple nail polish as Nesta likes that, hair conditioner, and last of all some Häagen-Dazs pecan as I know it's Nesta's favorite. And some Flakes because they're Izzie's favorite and I can't forget her in all this. And Mum said we can send out for pizza. Excellent.

When I got home from the shops, I went to my computer and designed an invite on e-mail to send to both of them.

```
Dear Izzie/Nesta
  You are invited to a girls' night
at Lucy's house tomorrow night at six
o'clock. Bring: makeup bags, nail
polish, hair stuff, favorite CDs, and
yourselves. I've got the pizza and
ice cream.
  Love Lucy
```

I pressed the send button and waited for their replies.

If you want a friend,
be a friend.

ANGEL CARD

Chapter 9

Bor-ing
Sundays

I got up the next day and went to check my incoming mail.

Nothing. That's strange. I know for a fact that Izzie always looks to see if she's got any e-mails first thing in the morning. What's going on?

At eleven o'clock, I phoned Izzie's house. No reply. Only Mrs. Foster's message on the machine: "I'm afraid we're unable to take your call at present. Please call later."

I called Nesta.

"Hi, is that little Lucy?" said Tony.

Gulp. "Yes. No. Sorry. I mean yes but I'm *not* little," I said.

He laughed at the other end, "Okay. *Lovely* Lucy, then. You want Nesta?"

"Yes, please."

"Not here. She went off somewhere with some guy from your school. Michael I think he was called."

"Was Izzie with them?"

"Don't think so. Shall I tell her you called?"

"Please," I said. "Thank you."

"And, Lucy?"

"Yes?"

"I think small girls are cute," he said, then he hung up.

When did I get so polite? Please. Thank you. Sorry. So much for my dazzling conversation. He must think I'm stupid. Why didn't I think of something brilliant to say? He likes girls who are funny. I could have told him my Scottish joke.

What's the difference between Bing Crosby and Walt Disney?

Bing sings but Walt disn'y.

But he did call me lovely Lucy. And he thinks small girls are cute. Maybe there's hope after all.

Sundays. What to do? It's such a *boring* day. *And* it's raining.

I had a quick look at my homework. My project for Miss Watkins stared back at me from my desk.

What makes me "me"?

What are my interests? Tony Williams.

What do I want? To snog Tony Williams.

What are my goals in life? To snog Tony Williams.

What am I? Shallow I suppose, since those are my main goals. Probably not ones that will impress Miss Watkins or Mrs. Allen either.

Okay. Snog Tony Williams and bring about world peace. That sounds better.

What would I like to do as a career? Still dunno.

Never mind, we've got a week or so left yet. I'll think about it later.

I went downstairs and flopped on the sofa in front of the television. Steve and Lal were squabbling over the channel changer. Steve wanted to watch a video of *The Matrix* and Lal wanted to watch *another* repeat of *Star Trek*.

I couldn't be bothered to join in and stake my claim. There was nothing on I wanted to watch anyway. Where was Izzie? I hope she hadn't gone off doing something with Nesta without me again.

"What can I do?" I asked, going into the kitchen where Mum was busy preparing some sort of weird nutloaf thing for lunch.

"Homework?" said Mum.

"Done it," I lied.

"Tidy your bedroom?"

"Boring . . . I've got *nothing* to do. . . ."

"Well I don't know," she said. "Just don't mope about under my feet. Anyway, I thought you were going to make some clothes. Why not make a start?"

I spent the rest of the morning rooting through bags of assorted jumble from the cupboard under the stairs. Most of it rubbish by the look of it, all sorts of stuff that Mum's collected over the years. Izzie says it's because she's Cancerian and they hate to throw stuff away. She's certainly right in Mum's case. There are clothes in here from when I was a baby.

Dad got up from reading his papers in the living room. "Time for a cup of tea!" he declared. He always says it like it's a really exciting thing. A sensational world event. TIME FOR A CUP OF TEA.

On his way to the kitchen, he spotted the baby clothes lying on the carpet. "Oh. Ahhhh," he said and picked them up and took them in to show Mum. They stood in the kitchen like a couple of dopes, all misty-eyed, looking at the tiny pink cardigans and miniscule blue booties.

"Our little baby," said Mum, gazing softly at me.

"It seems like only yesterday," said Dad, looking at me, "when you were still in nappies."

"*Errgh,*" I said. "Stop it."

"Maybe we should have another," said Dad.

I put my fingers in my ears. Yuk. I don't even like to think about it.

Suddenly I spied a box jammed in at the back of the cupboard and hauled it out.

I couldn't believe my eyes when I opened it. It was full of old dresses. I don't mean old like worn out, I mean old in that they looked like they'd been kept for decades. Fabulous fabrics, a velvet wrap, crêpe blouses with tiny little tucks and pleats, beautifully sewn, an evening gown with exquisite beading, a top with sequins. Satin, silks. I felt like I'd hit the jackpot.

"Mum," I called. "Whose are these clothes?"

Mum came to look at the heap of clothing I'd piled out on the hall floor.

"Oh, those. Those were your grandmother's. I used to wear them in the Sixties." She picked up a gorgeous pale lilac crêpe jacket. "I haven't looked at these in years. . . ."

"What are you going to do with them?" I asked.

"I don't like to throw them out . . ." she said.

"Supposed to be good Feng Shui, isn't it?" called Dad. "Clear your clutter and all that."

"I don't suppose I'll ever wear them again," Mum laughed. "But they're not exactly your style, are they? Maybe I could take them down to the secondhand shop or even to a costume shop for people to use in the theater."

I held my breath and asked, "Can I have them?"

"What on earth for? Are you doing a production at school?"

"Not exactly," I said. "It's just, I *think* I can do something with them."

♥ ♥ ♥

I piled the contents of the box and bags out on to the floor and started sifting through. Some of it was junk. Cable knit sweaters that had gone hard. T-shirts with paint all over them. But Grandma's stuff was a treasure trove.

I made a heap of the clothes I wanted and carted them upstairs with the sewing machine. Then I leafed through a couple of magazines for good designs and set about cutting, chopping bits off, hemming, and reshaping.

After a few hours, Mum appeared at my door. "What are you doing? We're all wondering where you've disappeared to."

"Creating," I said with a flourish, showing her what I'd done so far. "A short black velvet cross-over skirt and . . . my *pièce de résistance* for special occasions."

"Lovely," said Mum, feeling the material. It was powder blue lined chiffon with tiny pearls sewn all over it. "Isn't this from one of the evening gowns?"

"Yes. It was so easy to make, as it's only a sheath dress and got no sleeves, just the back and front sewn up at the sides. It's like one I saw Jennifer Aniston wearing in one of the mags."

"Oh, try it on, let me have a look," said Mum.

It fit like a glove.

"Very pretty," said Mum. "And it looks really professional."

"I doubt if anyone makes material like this any more. And I bet Nesta won't have anything like it from Morgan this time."

"Are you still worried about Nesta?" asked Mum.

"Not really. I've decided to make more of an effort with her. In fact, I'm making presents for both her and Izzie. I want to surprise them when they come over later."

I'd showed Mum the bandero top I'd started out of red sequin material for Nesta, then I was going to do a halter neck for Izzie with the leftover black velvet from the skirt.

Mum pulled a black ostrich feather out of the bag. "Why don't you use this to trim Izzie's top?"

"Good idea," I said. "I could hem it along the bottom."

By the time I'd finished, both tops looked so

good I was tempted to keep them for myself. But no, I wanted to give them something to show I can be a good friend.

"Lucy, phone!" called Steve from downstairs.

I was so absorbed in my sewing I hadn't even heard it ringing.

"Lucy," said Izzie's voice as I picked up the receiver. "I'm so sorry, I just called home and Mum said that you'd left a message."

"Oh right. And I sent you an e-mail too. I wanted to know if you and Nesta wanted to come over tonight for a girlie session."

"What, now?" said Izzie. "Isn't it a bit late?"

I looked at my watch. I couldn't believe it. It was nine thirty. I'd been sewing all day.

"Where have you been?" I asked. "In fact, where are you?"

I could hear music and voices in the background. It didn't sound like she was at home.

"Hold on," she said. "I'm going into the bathroom. I'm on the mobile."

"Where are you?"

"Lucy, please don't be mad when I tell you."

I immediately felt apprehensive.

"See Nesta went into Hampstead this morning and . . ."

Nesta again. I might have known she was with her.

"Yes, and?"

"Well she bumped into Michael Brenman and one of his mates and he asked her if she wanted to do something."

"Right . . ."

"Well she didn't want to be hanging around with two of them. She really likes Michael and wanted a bit of time on her own with him so she called me on her mobile and *begged*, begged me to go and meet them. Please understand, Lucy, we didn't mean to exclude you, but we couldn't ask you as well. I mean, we'd have looked like a right load of twerps if we'd all turned up."

"I know," I said grimly. "Two's company, three's a crowd."

"No. It's not like that, not exactly," said Izzie. "In fact, I wish you had come as well. I've got lumbered with Michael's mate. We're back at his house and he's a right Kevin. I'm going home in a minute if I can drag Nesta away from snogging

Michael. I'd rather have spent the day with you honest, *honest,* Lucy. You're not mad, are you? I had to meet Nesta. As a friend. And I did spend all last week with you trying to meet the Mystery Contestant. I didn't want to let Nesta down. . . ."

"Yeah, if you want a friend, you have to be a friend," I said, looking at the presents I had waiting for them and the face masks and makeup all laid out ready for the girls' evening.

"Yeah," said Izzie. "Oh, hold on a minute, Nesta's just come in. She says, come over to her house tomorrow after school. And oh, she says Michael is the worst snogger she's ever met. I suppose that means we can go home now."

Chapter 10

First
Kiss

Monday morning I overslept. I'd been up so late chopping up fab fabrics for future use, I was late for school and didn't get a chance to see Izzie or Nesta before lessons. I was feeling a bit wary of them both after Sunday.

Izzie gave me a little wave as I scrambled into my place in class, then in came Miss Watkins with a large shopping bag.

"I have a little homework for you all," she smiled mysteriously as she took what looked like three dozen eggs out of her bag. I could tell by her face it was going to be one of her mad ideas.

"Now then, Candice," she said. "I want you to hand out the eggs. One to each girl."

Candice did as she was told as we all looked at each other, mystified.

"I've been thinking about your career prospects," Miss Watkins said as she perched in her usual position on the desk corner. "There's one choice that none of you mentioned. It's full-time. It's demanding as well as rewarding. It means total, and I mean total, commitment. It's days, nights, and weekends. And sometimes no time off. Can any of you guess what I'm talking about?"

She looked around hopefully.

"Doctor," said Tracy Ford. "They're on call day and night sometimes."

"Okay, good," said Miss Watkins. "But they get holidays. No holidays with this."

"God," said Candice.

Miss Watkins laughed. "Not a job available to most of us," she said. "Any other suggestions?"

No one had a better idea.

"I'm talking about being a mother," she said. "And it's something you should all think about carefully."

Blimey, I thought. I'm only fourteen. Give me

a break. I haven't even got a boyfriend yet.

"Everyone always says it won't happen to me, but it only takes one time," Miss Watkins continued as half the class went scarlet and the other half went giggly, "and it can change your life for ever. I know you've all had classes about contraception, but this little exercise I want you to do will help you realize the responsibility you're undertaking if you don't use it."

My mind was boggling. Contraception? One night that can change your life for ever? Responsibility? What is she going to make us do with the eggs? I thought we were trying to decide our subjects.

"I want each of you to take the egg home," she continued as Candice placed one in front of each of us. "That's your baby for the week. I want you to bring it back next week in one piece, not broken."

Easy, I thought. I'll put it in the fridge.

"I want you to take it everywhere with you," said Wacko. "To the shops. To your friends' houses. To the bathroom."

What? Mad, she's completely mad.

She hadn't finished.

"And while we're at it, there's some leaflets on all the types of birth control available. I want you to pick one up from my desk at the end of the class so you can read through it at home. Any questions, ask your parents, or please come to me whenever you like."

Does she think we're sex mad in this class?

Clearly the answer is yes.

Nesta, Izzie, and I met up after school. With our egg babies. And our leaflets.

We read them on the bus to Nesta's house.

"It's weird, isn't it?" said Izzie. "One minute everyone's telling you not to grow up," she put on her snotty cow accent, "*to enjoy our youth.* Next minute, it's all grow up, decide what you want to be, and think about babies."

"I know," said Nesta. "But she must think we're a right load of plonkers if we don't know all about contraception by now."

"So what's oral contraception, then?" I asked.

"Talking your way out of it," said Nesta.

"You only have to say one word," said Izzie. "No."

I got the feeling neither of them had a clue. Best

to ask Mum. She's always too happy to fill me in on all the gory details.

"This coil thing sounds painful," I said, scanning the leaflet. "It goes in your womb. *Urgggh*."

"More painful for him more like," giggled Izzie. "Imagine, what if his thingy touches it, bd*OING . . . argghhhhh!*"

Once we started laughing we couldn't stop.

"My brothers found Mum's maxi pads once. Of course they didn't know what they were," I said. "Lal put one on over his head then pretended that he was a brain surgeon."

"When I was little I found my mum's. I used them as hammocks for my dolls," said Izzie. "She hid them after that."

"My mum uses a diaphragm," said Nesta, reading her leaflet. "I found it in her bedside drawer when I was about eight and thought it was a toy frisbee. So we had *the conversation*, you know, when they get all embarrassed and tell you the facts of life."

"The whole business sounds very messy to me," I said.

"Not as messy as having a baby," said Izzie, getting up suddenly and screeching. "I've just sat on mine."

Egg yolk dribbled off the bus seat on to the floor and that set us off laughing again.

"Egg on your face," sang Nesta, "egg on your face . . ."

"Not my face," grimaced Izzie, wiping yolk from her skirt. "Oh, my poor baby."

"Can't make an omelette without breaking eggs," I said.

"Oh, oh," moaned Izzie. "I'm a terrible mother. Look at you two. You've still got yours."

"I know," I said, looking at Nesta. "And I know exactly what we should do with them."

"What?" said Nesta.

"Let's go home and boil them."

"Great idea," said Nesta.

Somehow I don't think any of us are ready to be mothers just yet.

When we got to Nesta's, she made us big cups of frothy coffee on her dad's cappuccino maker and we went into their gorgeous living room. No sign of Tony.

"So why was Michael such a rotten snogger?" I asked Nesta. I was intrigued to know what a rotten snog was, not having being snogged at all so to speak.

"Onions," she said. "He'd had a hot dog. And it was all sloppy. Wet."

Sounded awful. "Have you snogged many boys?" I asked.

"Not really," she said. "About seven."

Seven? She's so experienced!

"The best was Alessandro," continued Nesta dreamily. "I met him last year when we were in Tuscany. He did it fabulously. Soft. Tender. Why? How many have you snogged?"

True to form, I went red. "None," I said. "I've never seen anyone I liked."

"Except Mystery Boy," said Izzie. "Don't forget him."

"How many have you snogged?" asked Nesta, turning to Izzie.

"Two," she answered. "Peter Richards when I was seven, so I don't suppose that counts. And I can't really remember how it was. And Stuart Cameron last year. He was okay, but he kept trying to grope me as well and I didn't really fancy him. No, I'm waiting for someone special. Not one of the local nerds, thank you very much."

Just at that moment, Tony appeared with a huge grin on his face. Oh, God. He'd been in the house all the time. How much had he heard?

He came in and flopped on the sofa next to me. "The art of kissing," he said. "My speciality."

"You wish," said Nesta. "What do you know? Nothing."

"More than you think, actually." He turned to me. "Never been kissed, eh?"

Red turned to scarlet turned to purple.

"Leave her alone," said Izzie.

"I was just going to offer to show her how it's done," said Tony. "Then she'll have something to measure it against in the future."

Aaarghhhh. I didn't know what to do. What to say. He was sitting so close. His long gorgeous legs in jeans stretched out in front of me. And he smelled nice, clean, not like Michael Brenman's overpowering pong. My breathing went all funny like someone had just pulled a belt across my chest.

"Yeah, she'll know what it means to be kissed by a huge show-off big-head . . . ," started Nesta.

"You want to try?" he said, turning to Izzie.

She tossed her hair. "In your dreams."

So he turned back to me.

"Lucy. Do you want to learn from the Master?"

"The Master . . . ," guffawed Nesta.

This only seemed to egg him on. He tucked a strand of hair behind my ear, tilted my face up to his, and looked into my eyes. My insides melted into warm honey.

"Tony . . . ," warned Nesta.

"Close your eyes . . . ," he whispered.

"TONY . . . ," Nesta again.

Too late. He was kissing me. I didn't care that Nesta and Izzie were there. My first kiss. Little firecrackers were exploding inside me. Nice. Very nice.

Suddenly a hand grabbed him by the back of his shirt. "In the kitchen," said Nesta harshly. "NOW."

He laughed and got up to follow her.

Izzie looked at me as they disappeared. "You okay?"

I nodded. I giggled stupidly. Okay? I was in heaven.

"The cheek of him," said Izzie. "Who does he think he is?"

"Just going to the loo," I said and crept out into the hall.

I could hear Nesta's voice in the kitchen. "You stay away from her, do you hear?"

My heart sank. *Why* was she saying that to him? He'd kissed me, surely that meant he liked me, and now she was ruining everything again. Why should he stay away from me? I didn't want him to. Not now.

There was only one thing for it. I'd tell Izzie and Nesta that he was my Mystery Contestant. And I was very happy to kiss him.

The doorbell rang and Tony came out of the kitchen. As he went to answer it, he gave me a wink.

Nesta obviously thought I wasn't good enough for him. But he did like me. I knew he did. He couldn't have kissed me like that if he didn't. Why did she always have to spoil everything?

Standing at the door was one of the prettiest girls I've ever seen, tall with long auburn hair and all dressed in black.

She pecked Tony's cheek, gave me a hands-off look, and followed him down the hall into his bedroom.

Just before he went in he turned back and grinned. "Homework," he said, then disappeared.

"His girlfriend," said Nesta, appearing at the kitchen door.

And more kissing lessons, if you ask me.

"Come on," said Nesta. "Let's go and make a plan for meeting that boy you like."

"Lucy, you look awful," said Izzie as I went back in.

I felt awful.

"It's Tony's fault. I could kill him," said Nesta.

"She's very pretty, that girl," I said.

"She must be completely thick," said Nesta, "to be going out with him."

"I know he's your brother," said Izzie, "but he *is* a bit big-headed."

"Understatement," said Nesta. "Nobody in their right mind could possibly fancy him."

Something told me this wasn't the best moment to tell them that Tony was the MC.

Has life ever, ever been worse? Just as I thought me and Nesta were getting on better, she tells her brother to stay away. And now I don't know what to think. Anyway, he has a girlfriend. A gorgeous girlfriend. What chance would I ever have against her?

How to be the Master Snogger,
by Tony Williams

Do
Have clean teeth and fresh breath
Vary the intensity of your kisses
Close your eyes
Leave her wanting more

Don't
Give gooey, wet, sloppy open-mouthed kisses
Kiss when you've been eating garlic, onions,
or tuna
Pin her down so she can't breathe
Kiss with your mouth shut tight

Chapter 11

Haircut From
Hell

"I'm going to get my hair cut," I told Izzie on the bus to school the next morning. "What do you think?"

I showed her all the pics I'd cut out of a mag last night showing different styles.

"Good idea," said Iz, pointing to one photo of a girl with cropped hair. "That would suit you. When are you going to get it done?"

"Tonight," I said.

"Wow, you move fast. Where?"

"The mall. Remember Candice had her hair cut last month? She told me if you go to the Aura school, where hairdressers go to get trained, they do it for free. They're always looking for volunteers to go along in the evenings."

"Great, me and Nesta will come as well. It's late-night shopping so we can get your hair cut then we'll have a mooch round. But what's brought this on? You've had your hair long for years."

"Angel Card," I admitted.

"An Angel Card told you to get your hair cut?"

"They were waiting for me when I got back from Nesta's last night. On the kitchen table. Waiting. Calling me. *Luuuucy, pick one.* I tried to resist but I couldn't help myself. In fact, I'm going to have to ask Mum to take them out of the house. I think I've become an addict. No resistance no matter what I tell myself or what kind of trouble they get me into. I see the pack and I *have* to pick one."

Izzie laughed. "They could start a group for addicts. ACA. Angel Cards Anonymous."

"Yeah, I'd get up and say, 'Hello. My name's Lucy Lovering and I'm an Angel Card addict. Let me tell you my sad story.'"

Izzie laughed again. "I'm a bit like that with the Net. Specially now I've found such a fab astrology site. So what did it say? The card last night?"

"No one can make you feel inferior without your permission."

"Wow. That's a good one," said Izzie. "I'll have to try it when I tell Wacko that I sat on my egg baby. But why did that make you want to get your hair cut?"

I wasn't sure how much to tell Iz. I'd gone home from Nesta's last night feeling like a complete failure. I didn't want to bore her to death with the list of things that make me feel inferior lately:

- Everyone knows what they want to be when they grow up but me.
- My lack of kissing experience.
- I only look twelve.
- Josie Riley's right. I am a midget.
- I'm as flat-chested as my brothers.
- I've never had a proper boyfriend. And now probably never will as the only one I like belongs to another.
- I can't even decide what color to paint my bedroom.

Inferior. Definitely.

"Time for a change," I said. "Remember that

horoscope you did for me that said it was time for a new me so don't resist? I thought what better place to start than with my appearance? I've been so busy thinking about inside stuff like who I am, strengths, weaknesses, all that sort of thing Wacko told us to think about, and it's got me nowhere. So I'm going to change the outside. Hair. My room. My clothes."

"Watch out world," grinned Izzie. "Sounds good to me."

After school we went straight to the mall. I sat in the hairdressing college reception with ten other volunteers. Girls behind an enormous glass desk registered everyone then told us to wait. It all looked very swanky. A vast marbled reception with the most enormous bouquet of white lilies in a vase. Everywhere were posters of Aura products and TVs up on the walls showing demonstrations. I've definitely come to the right place, I thought. I am going to look fantabuloso.

Nesta immediately started chatting to the girls on reception about where they got their models and how could she apply.

"Aries rising," said Izzie, watching Nesta flicking her hair about as she charmed them all.

"That's the leap before you look sign, isn't it?"

"Yeah. They have fantastic energy. Go for it is their motto, and never mind the consequences."

"But Nesta's a Leo," I said. "How can she be Aries as well?"

"That's what I've been discovering. Our individual horoscopes are far more complex than just having a Sun sign. Like Nesta. Leo is her Sun sign. Like yours is Gemini and mine is Aquarius. That's determined by the month you're born. Your rising sign is worked out by the *time* and place you're born. It changes every two hours."

"So people with the same Sun sign can be quite different personalities?"

"Exactly," said Izzie. "There's all sorts of factors—where your Moon is . . ."

"Moon? I thought you said Sun?"

"Astrology's a real science when you get into it. Everyone has a different Moon they were born under as well. That changes every two days. You have your Moon in Taurus."

"Is that good?"

"Fantastic. It's exalted there. The Moon rules how you are emotionally. And means you're very romantic. Taurus is ruled by Venus. It means you appreciate beautiful things."

"Have you worked out my rising sign?"

"Yeah. Cancer," said Izzie. "That means you're very sensitive. Emotional even, sometimes. Cancer is the sign of the crab and they can be a bit prickly on the outside but as soft as mush on the inside."

"So what does your Sun sign mean?"

"How you look, your general characteristics," said Izzie.

"Gemini's an air sign, the sign of the twins, isn't it?"

Izzie grinned. "Yep. So you have two sides to you. The public and the private."

"Schizophrenic, you mean? That explains how I've been feeling lately."

Izzie laughed. "Geminis are good at communication. Creative."

I stared at her with admiration. She really knows her stuff and I don't know why I ever worried about what makes me "me." I should just ask Izzie. She seems to know exactly.

"Lucy Lovering," called the girl at reception.

I got up and followed her, suddenly feeling apprehensive.

Izzie gave me the thumbs-up. "Meet you afterward."

I was ushered down a maze of corridors and into a small salon with a row of mirrors and chairs.

A girl with bright red hair and even brighter red lipstick came forward. She looked very young. She can't have been training that long. "Hi, I'm Kate and I'll be cutting your hair," she said. "Take a seat."

After that I might as well not have been there.

An older lady with long curly blond hair came in and they both stared at me for a while then played with my hair, tilting my head from side to side, frowning and tutting.

"Splits ends," said Kate with disdain. "Who cut it last?"

"Er, my mum," I said, feeling smaller by the minute.

Kate and her supervisor looked at each other knowingly. "Ah. That explains it."

"Take a seat at the basin," ordered Kate.

"Er, what are you going to do?" I asked as Kate shampooed me. "I've brought some pictures of how I'd like it to look. I've got them in my bag."

"We won't need those," said Kate. "Don't you worry, I know what I'm doing."

She led me away from the basin back to a chair then started snipping. I told myself to relax. Kate's hair looked fab and so did her supervisor's. I sat back, crossed my fingers, and closed my eyes.

A minute later, Kate's mobile rang. She had a quick look round to see if her supervisor was around, then seeing she wasn't, took the call. It went on like this for twenty minutes. Snip, snip, then she'd take a call. Some drama about a boy called Elliot. I could see she was getting in a panic about something he said, and didn't seem to be concentrating on my hair at all.

"Where were we?" she asked, coming back to me after the third interruption.

"You were on the back," I said. Then the phone went again.

"Won't be a mo," she said and disappeared again.

When she came back she was more flustered than ever, whatever was upsetting her, she seemed to be taking it out on my hair. Snip, snip, chop, chop.

I stared at my reflection in horror. My hair was gone. Cut or rather hacked bluntly to my neck and it didn't look even. It was *awful*. I felt myself go red and I wanted to cry.

By now, Kate was busy with the hairdryer, blowing and pulling.

"Ouch, that hurts," I said as she yanked a piece of hair then almost burned my scalp with the dryer.

"Got to get a move on," she said. "Got to get out quick. *Major* drama."

I didn't care about her major drama. I had one of my own. She'd totally ruined my hair.

When she'd finished blowing, she stood back to look at her work. I looked younger than ever. Nine. Eight. A baby. Oh no. What has she done?

By the look on her face, she didn't like what she'd done either.

"Are you pleased?" she asked, while shoving her things in her bag.

"It, er, looks a bit uneven," I said.

"That's the look," she said. "Very Meg Ryan. And those split ends had to go. It can be a bit of a shock if you've had long hair for a while. You'll get used to it."

Then she put on her coat and scarpered.

A moment later, the supervisor came back in and looked surprised that Kate had gone. "Where's your cutter?" she asked.

"Dunno," I said. "Gone."

"That girl is dizzy," she said crossly then she examined my hair. As she looked the frown on her forehead deepened. "If you don't like it," she sighed and looked at her watch, "come back another night and we'll restyle it for you."

No way, I thought. I'm not coming back here. Why did I have to get the cutter who was having some sort of relationship crisis? If only she'd looked at my pics. I looked a disaster.

Izzie was waiting for me in reception. I could tell by her face that she hated it too.

"I know," I said, feeling my eyes fill up again. "It's awful, isn't it?"

"It's different," she said, then saw my stricken face. She put her arm round me. "It'll grow back."

What? In five years. How could I have been so

stupid? Thinking that if I chopped my hair off suddenly I'd grow confidence. Look amazing. Now I looked worse than ever.

Izzie sighed. "I *am* sorry, Lucy. Look, Nesta's waiting for us so let's get out of here. Come on, we'll go and meet her then get a cappuccino."

"I can't go anywhere looking like this," I said. I wanted to get on the bus and go home and hide under the duvet until my hair had grown back.

"I said we'd meet her in the John Lewis lingerie department," said Izzie. "She's trying on Wonderbras."

"On no, please. I want to go home."

"Five minutes," said Iz. "Then we'll go."

We made our way into John Lewis and up to the first floor. Everywhere I looked I saw girls with lovely long hair and in mirrors that seemed to be on every wall, I saw me looking like a bird had built a straw nest on my head.

Nesta was waiting for us waving three bras in her hand.

"Oh," she said when she saw my hair.

"Yeah. Oh," I said.

"I like it," she lied.

"I have to go home for ten years," I said.

"But I've got a bra for you to try. I've picked one for each of us."

"I can't," I said. "I have no chest. And no hair."

"That's what's so wonderful about the bras," said Nesta. "No matter what size you are they make you look fab." She looked me up and down. "They give everyone an amazing cleavage."

"Come on, Lucy," said Izzie. "It'll be fun. You need cheering up."

They dragged me into the changing room and Nesta handed us our bras.

Reluctantly I took mine and went into a cubicle. A strange face looked back at me from the mirror. If I didn't know who I was before, I certainly didn't know who this was staring back at me. And the back of my neck felt cold.

"Wow," screeched a voice from next door. "It makes me look enormous." I popped my head round Izzie's curtain and, despite my hair, I couldn't help laughing.

"Hello, boys," she giggled.

"Aruba, aruba," I said. "Those things look like lethal weapons. *The Guns of Navarone*."

Izzie pulled a face. "My mum'd never let me wear it. You know what she's like."

"Ready!" called Nesta from the other side. We stuck our heads into Nesta's cubicle. She'd chosen a red satin one and though her bust is nothing like as big as Izzie's, the bra gave her a great cleavage. I decided I *would* try mine on. If they had this effect on Izzie and Nesta, it was bound to help me.

I went back to my cubicle and, avoiding looking at my hair, I stripped off and put on the bra. Outside I could hear Izzie and Nesta laughing their heads off about something.

"You ready?" called Izzie, then stuck her head in.

Tears were welling up in my eyes again.

"Oh, Lucy, don't cry . . . ," said Izzie.

I couldn't help it and now I'd started I couldn't stop. The dam burst and all the tears I'd been fighting back for weeks suddenly came pouring out. The more I looked at my reflection, the more I sobbed. I looked like a little girl in her mother's bra. A little girl with a really bad haircut.

Nesta put her head round the cubicle curtain and when she saw my face came in. "Lucy, whatever's the matter?"

I sat on the stool in the cubicle. "My bra doesn't fit," I sobbed.

"It's only a bra," said Nesta softly.

That made it even worse. "I know, it's not really that," I said, quickly putting my clothes back on. "It just seems nothing fits. Nothing. I don't fit. And this stupid bra is just the last straw."

I looked worse than ever now as my nose had gone red and my eyes were all swollen and puffy.

"I'm pathetic," I said.

Izzie and Nesta exchanged worried looks.

"I don't fit here. I don't fit at school. I don't know what I want to be when I grow up."

I looked at the two of them, both gorgeous with long glossy hair and fabulous cleavages. "And now you two are best friends and there's no room for me anymore."

Before they could say anything or get dressed, I ran out of the store and caught the bus home.

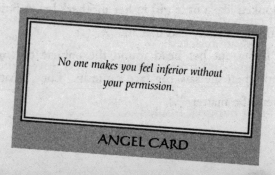

No one makes you feel inferior without your permission.

ANGEL CARD

Chapter 12

Inflatable
Bras

When I got home, everyone was eating supper.

Four faces stared open-mouthed at me from the kitchen.

"What've you done to your hair?" cried Lal.

Wrong response, I thought. But I knew there wasn't a right one.

I ran upstairs and hid under my duvet. Minutes later, Mum knocked.

"Come and have something to eat, love'" she said.

"Not hungry," I called.

Five minutes later, Dad knocked. "It's not so bad, love. We don't care what you look like. Come down and have your supper."

"You've got more hair than I have," I cried. "It's not fair!"

Then Steve tried. "Lucy, come down. *Buffy*'s on."

"Go away," I said. I didn't want to watch "*Buffy the Vampire Slayer*". All the girls in it had long fabulous hair.

Then Lal knocked. "I've got something for you," he said, then pushed his Beatles wig under the door. Ha ha, very funny. Not.

The clothes I'd made were lying on the chair at the end of my bed. I put them straight in the wastepaper bin. What had I been thinking of? They were rubbish. It doesn't work to try and change the outside if the inside isn't right. And my inside feels definitely not right.

I looked at my awful hair in the mirror again. I pulled at the roots, willing it to grow like the doll I had when I was five. You just tugged the hair and it came straight out right down to her waist. Why wouldn't mine do that? I couldn't even tie it up any more so that no one would notice what a strange style it was. So sticky-outee. I felt miserable.

And Izzie was right: I did have two sides as a Gemini. There were definitely two in me, both driving me nuts.

One part was completely freaked. My hair, my hair, I can never go out again. The other side was saying you selfish, petty, pathetic thing. Think about all the starving people in Africa. What does your stupid hair matter when there are war and famines?

Where did *that* voice come from? I know. Our headmistress Mrs. Allen. How did *she* get in my head?

I think I may be going mad. Completely. What makes me "me"? I am a nutter. Completely and utterly barking mad. And ugly.

At eight thirty, the doorbell rang.

"Lucy, it's for you," called Mum.

"Not in," I called back.

I heard a knock on the door.

"Lucy," said Izzie's voice. "It's me and Nesta."

I hid even further under the duvet as the door opened and they both trooped in.

"Luce, come out. Nesta has an idea."

I stuck my face out of the covers as both of them sat on the end of the bed.

"I spoke to Mum," said Nesta. "She has someone come to the house to do her hair every other week. She's coming tomorrow. She's really good, Lucy. She could fix yours."

"But I haven't got any money," I said. It was hopeless.

"Me and Iz have thought about that. We know you get less pocket money than us and we'll club together and we'll pay."

Both of them were looking at me with such kindness, it set me off again. Blub, blub. What *is* the matter with me these days?

"We thought you'd be pleased," said Nesta, looking puzzled.

"You're being nice to me," I sobbed. "Don't be nice to me. And I'm so selfish when there are wars and everything."

They both laughed.

"You're not responsible for the whole human race," said Iz. "Not yet anyway."

"I wanted to say something else," said Nesta,

looking embarrassed suddenly. "I never meant to take Izzie from you. It's just, I thought you didn't like *me*."

"But you always seem to want to be with Izzie . . . ," I began. "And I know I don't look old enough for some things you want to do like the cinema and hanging out with Sixth Formers and . . ."

"Those things don't matter. And I realize we shouldn't have gone without you that time. I really like you, Lucy. I want to be friends with Izzie *and* you. If you'll let me."

"But what about your brother? I thought you told him to stay away from me because you didn't like me."

"NoOO. Only to protect you, Lucy. Not because I don't *like* you. You don't know my brother. He thinks he's Casanova. A different girl every week. Once the challenge is over, he dumps them. We've only been in London a few months and already he's left a trail of broken hearts. I didn't want him to hurt you. That's all, honest."

"Really?"

"Yeah. I really *do* like you, Lucy, and want to be friends."

Tears filled my eyes again. "I'm so sorry," I said. "I don't seem to be able to stop crying. Just lately, I've felt I don't fit anywhere."

"My mum says it's our hormones running riot," said Izzie.

"I went through a time," said Nesta, "where we lived before. I was the only dark-skinned kid in our school. I *really* felt I didn't fit. . . ."

"So how did you handle it?"

"Decided I'd be proud I was different even if some days I didn't feel it. I toughed it out. I know sometimes that's all people see and they think I'm stuck up. But here in London, it's all been so different. Meeting you and Izzie. I feel I've got really good friends for once. And your mum and dad. You're so lucky. . . ."

"But yours are so glamorous . . . ," I began.

"Yeah, they're okay, but they're never there. Always working. That's why I love coming back to yours. It's so comfy and your brothers are great. I feel at home here. Everyone's made me feel so welcome."

"Except me," I said. I was beginning to see I'd misjudged her. She'd been trying to be my friend all along and I hadn't let her near.

Nesta grinned. "I was hoping I'd win you round in the end. I don't give up easily."

Suddenly Izzie spotted the clothes spilling out of the wastepaper bin. "What are these?" she said, pulling them out.

"Actually those are some presents I had for you, but . . ."

"Wow," said Nesta, seeing the red sequin top. "Where have you been hiding these? Why haven't you ever worn them?"

"Do you really like them?" I asked, getting out from under my duvet.

"They're fantastic," said Izzie, holding the clothes up and examining them. "Where did you get them?"

"I made them."

"You're kidding," said Nesta. "They look really expensive. Like designer stuff."

"Actually," I said. "I made that red one for you. And the black one's for you, Izzie."

In a second they had stripped off and put their presents on.

"Ohmigod," said Nesta, admiring her reflection in the mirror. "This is absolutely brilliant. I can't believe it. It's perfect."

It did look good, the red against her dark skin.

"This is the best thing I've got," said Izzie, twirling around in the halter neck. "Can we really have them? I just love it—and the ostrich feather trim. Mucho sexy."

I was glowing with pleasure. "I was going to chuck it all out. After today . . ."

"NoOOO, you mustn't," said Iz, seizing the blue dress I'd made for myself. "God, this fabric is amazing. All the little pearls. Put it on."

I put on the dress and both of them ooh-ed and aah-ed. It did look good as long as I didn't look above my neck.

"It fits like a glove," said Izzie, then laughed. "See, *something* fits!"

"Might look better if I had boobs," I said, thinking back to the lingerie department.

"Don't be mad," said Nesta. "They'll grow soon enough. And if they don't, you can always have silicone."

"Silicone! I'm four*teen*."

"Well what I mean is, at least you can do something about having no chest. Bras, uplifts. Not like my feet." She pulled off her trainers. "Look. Massive. Horrible. I can never get shoes to fit."

I couldn't believe it. Nesta wasn't perfect after all.

"That's nothing," said Izzie. "Try having my thighs. Both of you have such slim legs and I've got great whoppers. And short stubby ones at that. I can never get jeans to fit."

I felt so happy. Nesta and Izzie both had complexes. Why had we never talked about it before? I thought I was the only one who felt the way I did.

Hurrah. We're all mad.

Suddenly Izzie and Nesta started grinning like maniacs.

"What?" I said, suspicious. "What are you two up to?"

"Are you feeling better, Lucy?" asked Nesta, producing a package from her bag.

I nodded warily.

"Good, because we got you a little present as well," said Izzie.

"Something you really want," said Nesta.

Something I really want? My mind filled with

images of CDs, books, makeup I've had my eye on. What great friends.

Nesta giggled as she handed me the package in a carrier bag.

I put my hand in the bag and pulled out "the present."

Izzie and Nesta collapsed on the bed laughing as I looked at what looked like a bit of wrinkled pink plastic. "It's for your, er, your chest problem."

An inflatable bra. I started laughing and Izzie blew into the hole in the bra to inflate it. A perfect 34C.

"Put it on, put it on," she said.

I had to comply and shoved the bra up under my dress then stood in front of the mirror and turned to profile.

Nesta and Izzie made long wolf whistles.

"Pamela Anderson eat your heart out," I said, strutting and wiggling round the room. "*Baywatch* here I come. Yeah, thanks girls, like *very* funny."

Chapter 13

Pop Star
Names

We are the Three Musketeers. One for all and all for one.

Izzie brought her wet-look gel with her on the bus the next morning and Nesta plastered it on to my head.

"There, that's better," said Nesta, slicking my hair away from my face. "It's stopped it sticking out and you can't see it's all uneven any more. Then tonight, we'll get you sorted at home."

When we got off the bus, we headed straight for the corner shop. We had Wacko first lesson and it was hand in the egg baby day. Half our class were in the store. All buying free range eggs.

"Well done, girls," she said, when we all put the eggs on her desk. "I hadn't expected half of you to bring them back in one piece."

Everyone looked at the floor so we wouldn't catch each other's eyes and start laughing. Then Wacko said she wanted us to get into groups and discuss how far we'd got with our What-makes-me-"me"? project.

Just as things were going well, she had to bring *that* up again.

Izzie, Nesta, and me got into a group and stared at our files.

"Let's put in our pop star names," said Nesta.

"Pop star name?" I asked.

"Yeah, like a stage name. You take the name of your first female pet and your mother's maiden name and *voilà*, your pop star name. Boys pick the name of their first male pet."

I thought for a second. "Our first cat was

Smokey," I said. "And my mum's maiden name is Kinsler. So Smokey Kinsler."

"Takes all sorts, darlin'," said Nesta huskily.

"Hubba hubba," said Izzie. "Here's Smokey an' she's smo-oking tonight. Mine's Zizi. Zizi Malone."

"Mine's Sooty Costello," laughed Nesta.

"But Williams is your name," I said.

"I know, my mum kept her name and I use that instead of Dad's. So I'm using *his* maiden name. Sooty Costello. I like that."

"Perfect," I said.

"Let's put in our Mills and Boon writer names too," said Izzie.

"How do you do that?" I asked.

"You take your middle name and the name of the street where you first ever lived," said Iz.

"Suzanne Lindann," said Nesta.

"That works," said Izzie. "Mine's Joanna Redington."

"Mine's Charlotte Leister," I said, getting into it. "And we could put our death meals in too. It might come in handy if the aliens ever arrive and we have twenty-four hours before the world blows up."

"A death meal being?" asked Nesta.

"Your last meal ever on earth, stupid, like, if you know you've only got a few hours left."

That set us off dreaming for a while. All the lovely things we could eat and not have to worry about the calories or dieting.

"Chips, a burger, and Häagen-Dazs pecan," said Nesta.

"Roast chicken and roastie tatoes and banoffi pie," said Izzie.

"Spaghetti bolognese and treacle pudding and custard," I said. "And chocolate. Lots of it."

Nesta sent a note round class when Wacko wasn't looking. By the end of the lesson we had everyone's pop star names.

A good lesson methinks. And I suppose I'm getting clearer on the What-makes-me-"me" front. I'm Gemini with Cancer rising and the Moon in Taurus. I am an air sign, the sign of the twins. I am Smokey Kinsler, pop star queen or possibly Charlotte Leister, romantic novel writer.

Well, it's a start.

I looked up at Wacko and wondered if she would be impressed with our hard work.

"Lucy Lovering," she said, seeing me staring at her. "Stop sniggering."

She's picking on me. Do I care? No.

In the afternoon we all had to pile on to the school bus for an outing to the Tate Modern. Worse luck, some of the Year Eleven girls had come along to help "look after us."

As we took our seats at the back of the bus, Josie Riley came down the aisle and stood threateningly over Nesta.

"Hear you've been trying to cop off with Michael Brenman," she said.

Nesta immediately stood up. "It sounds like English but I can't understand a word you're saying," she said, going into her Scary Spice persona.

Now Nesta is definitely someone who doesn't give *anyone* permission to make her feel inferior. She's five foot five and Josie's at least three inches smaller.

Josie backed away then saw me giggling and turned to me. "What happened to your hair? Whatever look you're going for, you missed."

Izzie stood up next to Nesta. "If I throw a stick, will you leave?"

Josie turned on Nesta again. "You think you're it, don't you? Well let me tell you something. Michael Brenman is mine and I'd appreciate it if you'd stay away."

"Thank you, I will," said Nesta. "And as for Michael being *yours*, may I say we're all refreshed and challenged by your unique point of view. Anyway you can have Michael Brenman, I'm not interested, he kisses like a whelk."

Josie's mouth dropped open. "He *kissed* you? What does he see in a kid like you?"

Nesta stuck her nose in the air. "I'm really easy to get along with once you lesser people learn to worship me," she said.

Josie's mouth shrank to resemble a cat's bottom and by this time, I was on the floor laughing.

"One for all and all for one," I said as she sloped off.

There are a million things to look at in the Tate Modern. On the bank of the river Thames, it's an enormous warehouse type building with loads of different floors, each one with room after room of remarkable oddities, some beautiful, some seriously deranged.

As far as our class was concerned though, there was only one room worth looking at. After an hour of trooping around and trying to make sense of it all, we all jammed ourselves into a tiny dark space where there was music playing. On the wall a film was playing of a man with a beard. A naked man, sort of hippie dancing in slow motion. His willy was flopping up and down in time to the music. Everyone was falling about laughing and Candice Carter went up to the wall and started dancing along with him. That made us laugh even more.

"Is this art?" said Mo Harrison.

"Well it beats *The Hay Wain*," said Nesta.

"I thought you had to be able to draw to be an artist," I said.

"Not any more," said Nesta. "My dad said anything can be art if you say it is."

Then Mr. Johnson came in and caught us. He took one look at the film and said, "Move along, girls, come on, move along. Plenty more to see."

"Oh, I don't think so," said Izzie, trying not to laugh. "I think we've seen it all."

Sometimes school is great.

Year Nine

	Pop star name	Mills and Boon name
Lucy Lovering:	Smokey Kinsler	Charlotte Leister
Izzie Foster:	Zizi Malone	Joanna Redington
Nesta Williams:	Sooty Costello	Suzanne Lindann
Candice Carter:	Duchess Black	Rebecca Park Mead
Joanne Richards:	Muffin O'Casey	Emily Belmont
Gabby Jones:	Lucky Nolan	Lavinia Rosemount
Jade Wilcocks:	Roxanne Bennie	Rosemary Milton
Mo Harrison:	Flossy Cable	Gabriel Westerly

And: Nesta went up to Miss Watkins and said she was doing some research into old names for her history project so we also have:

Miss Watkins:	Mango Malloy	Violet Laurier

A class full of potential pop stars and Mills and Boon writers. Excellent. Most excellent.

Chapter 14

The
Mystery Contestant
Revealed

My hair is fantabuloso. At last. Can life get any better?

Betty, that's the hairdresser, is my new best friend. She looked more like a mum than a trendy hairdresser, and at first I had my doubts as to whether she could repair the damage.

Nesta's mum was just off to do her newsreading shift having had her hair done. She looked ever so smart in a navy suit and silver jewelry, and I thought I'd be intimidated by her like I am by Izzie's mum, but she was really friendly. She took one look at what Kate had done and said to Betty, "Oh no, she wants it softer, feathered, layered, don't you think?"

I nodded, but just to be on the safe side I showed them the picture I'd cut out of the magazine.

"Exactly," said Mrs. Williams, looking at the photo. "Something to show off your lovely bone structure. And, Betty, run a few highlights through." She turned to me before going out of the door. "My present, Lucy. I know what it's like when your hair gets ruined."

Nesta's family is fab.

And off Betty went. This time I didn't look in the mirror until she'd finished, then when I did . . . Wow. It was fantastic. Spiky and short at the front and layered all over. Then she put some white blond highlights through the top. Even I had to admit that this time the cut really suited me.

"You look gorgeous," said Izzie. "It really shows off your cheekbones. Amazing."

"You look elfin," said Nesta. "Very Winona Ryder."

After Betty had gone, we had another look

through Mrs. Williams's interior design mags and I saw the room I wanted. Pale lilac. With powder blue paintwork.

"*Très chic*," said Izzie.

It was all coming together. My hair, my room, my friends.

It was time to ask Nesta my burning question.

"Nesta," I said gravely.

"Yes, oh gorgeous one?" she replied.

"You know Tony?"

"Yes," she laughed. "He's my brother."

"Why doesn't he live with his mum?"

Nesta went quiet. "She died. In a road accident when he was six months old. He never knew her. A year later, his dad met Mum, and, well, my mum's the only mum he's ever known, even though she's not really his mum physically."

"Where is he tonight?" I asked. I wanted him to see me with my new haircut. Looking fantabuloso.

"Some class after school, I expect," said Nesta. "He often stays late for one thing or another."

Suddenly Izzie clapped her hand over her mouth and gave me a strange look, "Ohmigod," she said. "OhmiGOD."

"What?" chorused Nesta and I.

"Tony," said Izzie. "*Tony*."

She knew. I *knew* she knew. I went purple and now she definitely knew.

"What?" said Nesta.

Izzie crossed her arms and looked at me as if to say, I'm not saying, are you going to?

I glanced at Nesta and decided I could trust her.

"What?" she said.

"Tony," I said.

"I know," she said. "Tony, Tony. *Tony* what?"

"A boy that we didn't see in Highgate because he stays late for classes after school?" said Izzie, waiting for the penny to drop.

Nesta thumped her forehead. "Except we *did* see him, didn't we? Obvious. Obviouso. Tony is the MC."

I nodded.

"And he made you kiss him," said Izzie.

"And I told him to stay away from you," said Nesta. "No wonder you hated me. Why didn't you say, Lucy?"

"I thought you'd tell him I fancied him and then I'd, I'd look stupid. If he knew I'd been waiting for him to come out of school, I'd look like a real desperado."

At that moment, we heard someone coming in the front door.

Oh, let it be her dad back from America, I prayed, but of course, Murphy's law, it was Tony.

"Hiya, everybody," said Tony. "Wow. Is that little Lucy? Hey, you look great. Gorgeous."

He came and sat next to me. "Want another kissing session?"

Nesta and Izzie just sat there gaping.

"*What*?" said Tony. "Why are you all staring at me? What? What's happened?"

Suddenly I got the giggles and couldn't stop. That set Izzie off then Nesta and soon the three of us were holding our sides laughing.

Tony got up and stomped to the door. "Girls. Sometimes you lot can be really juvenile."

"I thought he liked girls with a sense of humor," I said, still laughing.

"Not when it's directed at him," said Nesta. "And I won't say anything, about, you know, him being the MC, if you don't want."

"Thanks," I said. "I *don't* want."

"Anyway," said Izzie. "I reckon you could get anyone you want looking like you do now. Play the field a while."

"Ah, but I have been kissed by the Master," I said, giggling again.

"Then you owe it to yourself," said Izzie, "to see if anyone else can match up."

Chapter 15

Decisions,
Decisions . . .

"So girls," said Wacko a fortnight later. "Next week I want your subject choices in. You've all had plenty of time to think about it, so I expect your papers on my desk on Monday."

Eek. Double eek. I hadn't thought about it at all. Not for ages. I'd been too busy having a good time with Nesta and Izzie and making clothes and doing my bedroom.

We'd spent the last two weekends painting. Lal and Steve had helped and it looked fantastic. I chose lilac mist for the walls and, as I'd seen in the interior magazine, we painted the woodwork pale powdery blue. The room was transformed and looked much bigger, as well as cleaner and brighter.

Mum took me down to a market in the East End to look for fabrics for the curtains and cushions, but we didn't see any I liked at any of the stalls. Then we passed an Indian shop. Rolls of beautiful materials were spilling out on to the pavement. I had to stop. Lovely shimmering jewel colors with silver and gold borders.

"Mum, let's look in there," I said, pulling her in.

I found a roll of sky blue *sari* fabric with a silver embroidered border. It would look stunning against the lilac walls and it wasn't too expensive. We made our purchase then bought some lining and some curtain rails.

When I got home, Mum helped me do the curtains and we made them so that the lovely silver border was at the bottom. We even had enough to swathe some at the top. It was the finishing touch and made the room look floaty and soft.

The overall effect was lovely but had taken up all my spare time. Subject choices hadn't even got a look-at.

❤ ❤ ❤

Things were looking up on the boy front, too. When I go out with Izzie and Nesta now, boys look at me as well. And not just the nerdy ones that no one else wants. Some quite cute ones have given me the eye. But to my mind, no one came close to Tony.

I saw him a couple of times at Nesta's, but he ignored me. I don't think he had recovered from us all laughing at him. Then one evening, he came out of his room when I was going to the bathroom.

"*Psst*," he said. "Lucy, in here."

I followed him in and he shut the door. I stood there nervously wondering what he wanted. Then before I could say anything, he pushed me back against a wall, put my arms around his neck and kissed me. A long deep sensual kiss that went right down to my toes and back again.

Then he stood back. "So, do you want to go out some time?"

I remembered everything that Nesta had said about him. He likes a challenge then dumps the girl. Nesta said he'd even chucked the girl I saw there a couple of weeks ago. Izzie's words also went through my head. Don't be too easy. Boys like a challenge. Although it was very tempting, I took a deep breath and moved away from him.

"I don't know," I said. "I'll think about it."

He looked taken aback then shrugged. "Suit yourself."

Then he opened the door to let me out. "You're probably too young for me anyway."

But he was smiling as he said it.

Time was running out. Monday was D-day for Wacko and Saturday was the Clothes Show. When was I going to have time to choose my subjects? I got my file out and sat at the kitchen table with what I had done so far in front of me. Three lines.

"Lucy, shouldn't you be in bed?" said Mum. "It's almost eleven o'clock."

"We have to hand this in on Monday and I still haven't a clue what I want to do when I grow up. Too many choices. It's driving me mad."

Mum sat down at the table next to me. "I remember feeling the same," she said. "In fact even now I don't know what I want to be when I grow up."

"But you *are* grown up. And you have a job."

"Yes, but I still feel nineteen sometimes. There're always choices, aren't there? I mean, I know I have a job. I'm a psychotherapist. But that's not what I am. It's only what I do. Who I am is changing all the time and I could change my job any time I want."

"I wish I could decide on just one thing, never mind think of changing. It's such a nuisance."

"Choice isn't a curse, Lucy. It's a blessing. And there will always be choices. Every day, every week. They'll keep coming."

I groaned.

"There are easy choices, like do I want tuna pizza or four cheeses? Shall I paint my nails pink or purple? And there are the bigger choices, more serious stuff like career or relationships. And those choices will seem to keep changing depending on how you're feeling inside as well as how outside influences affect you."

"It all sounds so complicated,' I sighed. "Oh for an easy life."

"I'll drink to that," said Mum. "How are you getting on with that boy you like?"

"He says I'm too young for him. But it's not that. One of the girls he went out with, I thought she was sixteen but turns out she's the same age as me. I just look young for my age."

"You'll see that as a gift one day," smiled Mum. "It's a family gene; none of our family looks their age. Believe me, when you're thirty or forty you'll be glad you look younger. But for now, come on, up to bed. Sleep on it. You never know, it might all become clear in the morning."

Fat chance. I'll never be able to sleep. What if I pick the wrong subjects and regret it? I wish, I *wish* I knew what to do. Decisions, decisions, decisions.

Chapter 16

The Way is Clear

I made a special outfit for the Clothes Show. Halter tops are turning out to be my speciality and I ran one off out of some of the leftover *sari* material using the silver to make crisscross straps at the back. Then I made a gray crêpe wrap skirt to go with it.

I met up with Nesta and Izzie at the tube station. Nesta looked sensational wearing her black leather trousers and a short jacket. And I was so pleased to see that she had my red top on underneath.

Izzie was wearing a long hippie dippie outfit in purple with some amethyst jewelery she found at a stall in Camden.

The hall was heaving with people when we got there. We paid for our tickets then went to join the crowds wandering around the many stalls and shopping areas. Izzie was soon absorbed in a stall selling New Age lotions and crystals. Nesta was busy craning her head looking for talent scouts.

"Aren't they supposed to spot you, not the other way round?" I asked. "Just relax, Nesta. Enjoy yourself. The talent scouts will be doing just that: scouting."

We were wandering into one of the shops when I stopped in my tracks.

"What? Who have you seen?" asked Nesta.

I pulled Nesta behind a rail of clothes and pointed. There was Josie Riley and a bunch of her mates. Josie was flirting with a boy who was standing in the middle of them lapping up the attention. She was flicking her hair about and doing all that touchy feely stuff, brushing the boy's arm and looking deeply into his eyes.

It was Tony.

"Oh, don't worry, Lucy," said Nesta. "He may be a big-head, but he's not stupid."

I wasn't so sure. He'd said how much he liked

confident girls and Josie was certainly that. Plus he looked like he was really enjoying himself.

Suddenly Josie spotted us and gave us a sick smile and a wave.

"Want to go over?" said Nesta.

"Oh no," I said, darting behind another clothes rail. "I couldn't bear it if he likes her."

"Suit yourself," said Nesta. "Anyway he hasn't seen us."

There was so much to take in. Hours flew by as we tried clothes on, experimented with new eye colors and plastered ourselves with free samples of moisturizer and perfume.

Izzie wanted to return to one stall to have a toe ring fitted, so Nesta and I decided to go and watch one of the catwalk shows. We turned a corner and I walked smack into Josie.

"Ah, the midget," she said, then looked me up and down and laughed. "What have you got on? The Eastern look was out years ago. You look like an advert for curry in a hurry."

All her friends started laughing and suddenly my new found confidence failed me.

"She made those clothes herself and I think she looks fantastic," said Nesta, coming to my defence. "I don't suppose someone with your IQ could even sew on a button."

"Ahhhh," said Josie. "Made them yourself, did you? Poor thing. Can't afford new clothes." She did a twirl. "My mum brought my outfit back from Milan."

"There's a big difference between buying expensive labels and having style," said Nesta. "Lucy has style. Something you'll never, ever know about."

"And I suppose you do," said Josie, then smiled smugly. "Oh and Michael Brenman, you can have him. I've met someone much better."

Nesta shrugged. "Oh clear off, Josie, I'm not in the mood," she said, and tried to get away. But as she walked to the right, Josie and gang walked with her. She tried to walk to the left, but again they blocked her way. It was starting to feel uncomfortable as there were four of them and only the two of us, then Josie stepped forward and trod on Nesta's foot.

"Ow!"'she cried. I winced even though it wasn't

my foot. Josie was wearing high, spiky-heeled shoes.

"Oh *sorry*," said Josie insincerely. "Did that hurt?"

"Need a hand?' said a male voice.

We all turned. It was Tony. Josie and her mates sprang back straight away.

"No, I'm fine," said Josie, going all coy and girlie.

"Not you," he said, brushing her aside and putting his arm round Nesta. "You all right, Nesta?"

Josie looked shocked. Of course she couldn't know that he was Nesta's brother, and he was clearly the best-looking boy in the hall.

"We were just admiring Lucy's outfit," lied Josie, and her friends started sniggering again.

Tony turned to me. "Looking good, kiddo," he said. "Come on, girls, I'll buy you a cappuccino."

Josie obviously thought he meant her as well, as she trooped along after us.

He put his arms round Nesta and me and turned back to Josie. "Sorry, three's company. Four's a crowd."

Ha ha. That showed her.

"I thought you liked girls who are sure of themselves," I said as we walked towards the coffee bar.

"Do me a favor," he said. "Yeah, I like confident

girls, but I don't like the music turned up *quite* that loud if you get my meaning."

Tony. I think I'm in love.

As Tony went to find a table, Nesta and I queued up to get our drinks. As we stood waiting, I noticed the redheaded lady in front of us staring. I felt embarrassed and wondered if my homemade stitching was so obvious.

"Nice top," the woman said.

I blushed. "Thanks."

"Where did you get it?" she asked.

"I made it myself," I said.

The woman looked me up and down thoroughly. "I'm impressed."

"She made this top as well," said Nesta, doing a twirl for her.

"Really?" the woman said. "You've got a good eye. Simple designs always look the best."

Then she put her hand in her bag and pulled out a card. "Here. Remember me when you've finished college."

"College?" I said.

"I presume you are going to do fashion. Design?"

I was taken aback. I'd never thought of it. Then it felt like the clouds lifted. The way was clear.

"Yes," I grinned back at her. "Course I am."

"Well good luck and get in touch when you finish. I'm always on the lookout for fresh talent and innovative design."

Then she bought her drink and moved away.

Nesta took the card. "Ohmigod," she said.

"What?"

"That was Viv Purcell."

The name meant nothing to me.

"*The* Viv Purcell. She's one of the hippest designers around. Anyone who's anyone is fighting to wear one of her outfits."

I felt myself glowing with pleasure. She'd picked me out and told me to keep her card. And, best of all, she'd put her finger on the spot. What I want to be when I grow up. A designer. Of course, of *course*.

I spent the next hour cruising round in a rosy glow of happiness. Tony hung round with us for most of the morning and every time we spotted Josie and crew, she looked sick with jealousy. Especially when at one point, Tony put his arm round me.

When he was leaving, he winked and smiled at me. Maybe. I thought. Maybe one day. It wasn't over yet.

Of course Nesta got spotted by her talent scout. She stood out from the crowd like she always does and was approached by not one but two talent scouts who asked her to get in touch with them.

We went home, over the moon. Nesta, her head in the clouds with dreams about being a model. Me, over the moon because now I knew what made me "me." I knew what I wanted to be when I grew up. I'd be able to choose my subjects.

Later that evening, I sat working on my What-makes-me-"me"? project when the phone rang.

"Lucy, it's me," said Nesta. She sounded as if she'd been crying.

"What's the matter?"

"My mum," sobbed Nesta. "She won't let me phone the agencies."

"Why not?"

"She says I have to focus on my studies. My life is over. My one chance and she's ruining it all."

"Does she have to know?"

"Yes. That's just it. Both the scouts said if I go in to see them I have to take Mum with me."

"What does your dad say?"

"Same. I rang him in LA and he said I shouldn't even think about it yet. My life is over. What else can I do? You're so lucky you know what you're doing. And your mum and dad aren't likely to object."

I knew how she felt. Wow. Did I know how she felt.

"Nesta," I said, remembering what Mum had said. "There will always be choices. Always. Anyway, being a model isn't your only one. You can be an actress as well. And if you don't want to do that, you can join a model agency later. You're not going to lose your looks."

We chatted on for about half an hour and at the end Nesta said, "Thanks, Lucy. You're a really good friend."

As she put the phone down, I realized she was right. I am.

Lucy Lovering. What Makes Me "Me"?

My name is Lucy Lovering. I am a person that makes choices.

They change. I change. That's life.

Who am I? Astrologically, I'm Gemini with Cancer rising and the Moon in Taurus. That makes me the individual I am, but how I feel can change according to the stars and the sun and moon depending where they are in the sky.

At the moment I am four foot eight. And a half. That will change.

I like pepperoni pizza. That *might* change.

My favorite color is blue. That also might change.

My pop star name is Smokey Kinsler and my Mills and Boon name is Charlotte Leister. But I doubt if I will take up either of those names as I have other plans.

What are my interests? Art, design, fashion. I hate math and I hate science. I doubt if that will change, but you never know.

What are my strengths and weaknesses?

Strengths are making clothes, and design. And being a good friend.

Weaknesses, ice cream, Tony Williams, and any animal with sad eyes.

What would I like to do as a career? Easy. Design. Maybe fashion, maybe interiors. I'm told I have "the eye."

Best of all, I have two best friends. Izzie Foster and Nesta Williams.

That will never change.

Read all the books starring
Lucy, Izzie, and Nesta!

Mates, Dates, and Inflatable Bras

Mates, Dates, and Cosmic Kisses

Mates, Dates, and Designer Divas

(COMING SUMMER 2003)

BE SURE TO READ *ALL* OF THE ALICE BOOKS

Also check out Alice on the Web at
http://www.simonsayskids.com/alice
- Read and exchange letters with
  Phyllis Reynolds Naylor!
- Get the latest news about Alice!
- Take Alice quizzes!
- Check out the Alice books
  reading group guide!

"Naylor's funny, poignant coming-of-age series . . .
has continued to serve as a kind of road map for a
girl growing up today." —*Booklist*

Once upon a time is timely once again as fresh, quirky heroines breathe life into classic and much-loved characters.

Reknowned heroines master newfound destinies, uncovering a unique and original happily ever after. . . .

Historical romance and magic unite in modern retellings of well-loved tales.

✦✦✦✦✦

THE STORYTELLER'S DAUGHTER
by Cameron Dokey

BEAUTY SLEEP
by Cameron Dokey

SNOW
by Tracy Lynn

PUBLISHED BY SIMON PULSE